It was strictly a business proposal

Rachel waited impatiently for his answer. It was simple—why couldn't he see that?

"All right," Charlie said finally. "I guess I could—theoretically—agree to the proposal."

"Great! I'll get the medical team out here tomorrow to start the procedure. They can get it over with in a jiffy."

"Now, whoa," he objected. "Hold on a sec. I said I can see this being a reasonable idea—in theory. But when you come right down to it, I don't know if I can agree. Artificial insemination?"

"It's simple," Rachel said dismissively, "and by far the most scientific way of doing it. The ranches use the technique all the time."

"That's the trouble with all this research. Sure, artificial insemination is great for the rancher. And probably the cows don't mind in the least. But did anyone ever ask the bull what *he* felt about the situation?" Charlie looked directly into her eyes.
"No. If you want me to father your child, then we do it the old-fashioned way."

EMMA GOLDRICK describes herself as a grandmother first and an author second. She was born and raised in Puerto Rico, where she met her husband, a career military man from Massachusetts. His postings took them all over the world, which often led to mishaps—such as the Christmas they arrived in Germany before their furniture. Emma uses the places she's been as backgrounds for her books, but just in case she runs short of settings, this prolific author and her husband are always making new travel plans.

Books by Emma Goldrick

Yes, I know.'' Charlie chuckled again. ''Just *Her*.''
could almost hear the capital letters in *Her*. ''His
ghter? Little Rachel? I can't believe that. She was
a kid when my uncle wrote about her. Sent a picture,
Too bad Uncle Roger died before I could come and
out what he wanted. What is she—twenty—twenty-
''

You forget a lot of years,'' Frank said. ''And don't
her Rachel. She prefers to be called Hammond. I
d guess she might be all of twenty-nine or thirty by

'd like to see this harridan. Why don't we walk over
and drop in on her?''

Not me.'' Frank stepped a pace or two away almost
he were trying to put real distance between himself
Charlie Mathers. ''You must be crazy or something.''
Or something,'' Charlie agreed as he came to a halt
surveyed the yellow-brick monstrosity across the
. His lawyer stared at him as intently as he stared
e building. Charlie Mathers had spent five years
college in the stock market. Then he had put all
oney in trusts, turned its management over to his
r, and dropped out of sight. Now here he was, back
wo days from—wherever. Charlie Mathers. Just
clearing five feet eleven, but built like some bar-
conqueror, his hair down to his neck in unruly
ay. The neck itself a short, thick steel pillar laced
uscles.

hair had once been yellow blond. Now it was
d almost white by a tropical sun. In the warmth
Kansas springtime he was wearing a loose, well-
ports shirt, from which his arm muscles bulged,
ppy pair of pants. From a distance he appeared
ordinary but solid man; not until one came

BABY MAKES THREE
Emma Goldrick

Harlequin Books

TORONTO • NEW YORK • LONDON
AMSTERDAM • PARIS • SYDNEY • HAMBURG
STOCKHOLM • ATHENS • TOKYO • MILAN
MADRID • WARSAW • BUDAPEST • AUCKLAND

ISBN 0-373-03303-6

BABY MAKES THREE

Copyright © 1993 by Emma Goldrick.

This edition published by arrangement with Harlequin Enterprises B. V.

® and TM are trademarks of the publisher. Trademarks indicated with ® are registered in the United States Patent and Trademark Office, the Canadian Trade Marks Office and in other countries.

Printed in U.S.A.

CHAPTER ONE

"Look, Charlie," his forty-year-old lawyer an friend cautioned him as they idled along the across from the pyramid-shaped building t the magazine. "Things aren't the way they w uncle's day."

Charlie Mathers looked across the street an "You didn't have to say that, Frank. Who's for the Egyptian rococo monstrosity over the was never like this, was it?"

Frank Losen winced, and looked around to make sure nobody was listening. "*She's* re he murmured. "You wouldn't believe! Wa the boondocks, Rachel Hammond is publish of one of the nation's wildest scandal shee Libertyville is only a few miles from Top the print capital of the Middle West." Sa of pride that Charlie acknowledged by a "Her father was a tough cookie, if member. His daughter makes him look friar!"

"I'd believe almost anything after the Near East. It hardly matters, d make up all their news out of whol the old man have a son to inherit?

"A boy," Frank told him. "Litt drink the hard stuff at fifteen, ar cycle around a lamp post when h that left——"

5

closer did his actual size meet the eye. Everything not covered by hair or clothing was a deep sun brown. Except for those commanding deep blue eyes.

"And you won't just walk across with me," Charlie teased again. "After all, the Hammonds and the Mathers were once great neighbors."

"Sure. About a century ago," Frank said. "Yes, you did inherit from your uncle Roger, and included was forty per cent of the shares in the Hammond-Borgen Corporation, which includes the Bar Nine ranch, and that damn magazine. The *National Gossiper*, would you believe? And no, you don't get me into that—that bitch's lair!"

"She must be something." Charlie laughed. "Bitch? And you a staunch Methodist!"

"Listen to me, Charlie. You've got more money than I can count. Even the bank president tips his hat when you walk by. You don't *need* to know the Hammonds. Leave the sleeping dogs alone. You might get yourself cut off somewhere south of your hip pockets. And that's my last word on the subject!"

"Amen. Well, you go on back to your office, Frank. You've done a good job managing my money. I think I'll just leave it in your hands while I sniff around the town and edge my way back into civilization."

"That makes a lot of sense, old buddy. And I think I'll—run along."

"Yeah, why don't you?" Charlie encouraged. "I do believe somebody important is coming out over there." He turned around to offer some other comment, but by that time his lawyer, laden with forty years of worry and a heavy briefcase, had already disappeared.

That's what I need, Charlie told himself. Something intriguing to do. Something with a lot of—gentle adventure. Something where I can have some fun without being shot at! I don't intend to set foot in an F-15 cockpit for the rest of my natural life.

Women, that's the proper subject for a middle-aged man these days. Isn't thirty-four middle-aged? Women. But then I suppose the lady's as ugly as they come. Isn't that what sours a woman? Ugliness? Or lack of love?

A gray stretch limousine pulled up at the opposite curb. The double doors of the building swung open and two very large men came out cautiously onto the pavement. One looked like a misplaced basketball player; the other like King Kong in a business suit. The pair of them turned in a semicircle, searching opposite ends of the street. Unconsciously Charlie Mathers did the same. There was not another soul in sight—except for himself.

The men held a very short conversation, and then made a beeline for Charlie. You've been a long time away, Charlie thought, as he watched the pair move in his direction. Things really *have* changed.

"Hey, you," the Kong-type said. "Doin' somethin' special here, are you?"

"Nope. Just hanging around." Charlie Mathers had long been noted as a violent man, but this pair certainly wouldn't know his reputation. Sometimes his patience lasted for as long as ninety seconds. On his good days, of course.

"Something I can do for you?"

"Yeah. How about moving down the block a ways?" The bean pole spoke politely, but he kept pounding one big fist into the palm of the other with monotonous precision.

"Why is that?"

"Because Hammond's coming out, and she don't like gawkers. Move along."

"Well, I'll be damned." Charlie shook his head and smiled. "Just what I need. I've been aching to see this Hammond. And she's coming out right now?"

"Achin' you'll get," the gorilla said. "Seein' you won't."

"She's been shot at a time—or two," the taller man said. He sounded conciliatory, but his fist was still pounding into the palm of his hand, and making heavy popping noises as it did.

"Just move," the other growled, and reached one big hand out for Charlie's shoulder. A genial smile flashed across Charlie's face.

"Why, you two aren't being friendly at all," he crowed. In one friendly little swoop he lifted the hand off his shoulder and the gorilla off his feet and threw him about six feet, where he cannoned into his partner and left both of them sprawling in the gutter.

Rachel Hammond, twenty-nine years old and counting, paced her office one more time. The idiot who had designed the pyramid had long since been fired. Having your office at the top of such a structure gave you four windows, four slanting walls, and not much room for pacing. Rachel was a woman who needed pacing room. The elderly man sitting on the stiff-backed chair followed her with his eyes.

"Look, Elmer. I said dig up a little scandal, but I didn't mean in Libertyville, for heaven's sake. Who in the world gives a damn that someone on the town council is selling favors? Kill the damn thing. I want something juicy!"

Elmer Chatmas had been with Rachel's father, and her father's father, and was not about to run for cover. "There doesn't seem to be anything to meet the requirement," he said quietly. "We might do something with this thing over in Topeka in the city solicitor's office, but it's a little staid. Just an ordinary embezzlement."

"So jazz it up," she told him. "Add a couple of babes. Get a couple of leg pictures. You know the routine— 'CITY OFFICIAL STEALS TO SUPPORT SEX HABITS'—or something like that. Come on, Elmer, I've got an important appointment in fifteen minutes."

"Just make up a blatant lie?"

"Not a lie, Elmer. That's what we call creative journalism. You know what to do. We print the real news on page two, and save page one to make money enough to keep this old scow afloat. Now come on. Put the issue to bed!"

"I don't know how you do it," he said as he got up and gathered his papers together. "Whatever happened to that sweet little girl I used to dandle on my knee?"

The *sweet little girl* smiled at him. "Rachel Hammond?" she asked. "She grew up, Elmer, and found out that the world isn't round, it's crooked."

"What you need is a good man," the editor told her as he walked out of the room.

"Sure I do," she called after him. "But God isn't making any more of that model." The door swung shut, locking her in. A shiver ran up and down her spine. Of course it wasn't locked, only closed. Am I coming down with claustrophobia? Or chicken pox? She changed her route, and opened the door of the tiny bathroom adjacent to her office. The mirror lied to her.

She felt fifty years old; the mirror said twenty-nine. Her hand brushed through her mop of curls; blond beautiful curls, the mirror said. And blue eyes, with rose red cheeks to go with her pearly complexion. Fine white teeth, a sharp little nose, a determined chin, medium height, and a figure that would have sent Michelangelo into shock!

And soon I'll be thirty, she told herself ruefully. The woman who had appeared on the late-night talk show two months ago had hit it just right. Rachel Hammond could hear her biological clock ticking!

It was the sort of problem a woman might possibly discuss with her friends—if she had any. Or with her pastor—if she didn't think he was such a wimp. And that was the trouble. She wasn't interested in finding a "good man," someone who could dictate to her as her father had. What she wanted was a baby. Somebody you can dictate to? her conscience asked. "No, not that," Rachel muttered to the empty office. "Someone I could love and cherish. Someone who might love me back!" Which immediately ruled out any adult she could think of.

She hadn't been a success at loving during her own childhood. Her mother gave up the cocktail circuit just long enough to bear her, and then had died. Her father, once he discovered she was not a boy, had treated her like a misdirected parcel, come in the mail with no return address.

But not all of Rachel's education had been wasted. No matter how she squirmed around it, to have a baby you had to have a man. And that was the idea around which she had built her campaign. She trusted her doctor. A woman, of course. They had put their minds together, and finally had come up with a newspaper advertisement.

Wanted: strong, healthy male, willing to accept high-paying, short-term job.

"And that," Rachel had said, "will bring in a flood of strong, healthy, lazy males, willing to take my money for almost anything."

"So we'll say 'willing to participate in hazardous short-term experiment at high pay.'"

"That sounds more like it," Rachel had agreed. "And you'll screen them out?"

"Dr. Greenlaugh first. She's a psychiatrist. When she finds the ten best she'll send them over to me for a physical."

"A damn thorough physical," Rachel had added. "I don't want to get to the end of the search and find the guy can't—well, you know."

"I know," Dr. Saunders had agreed with a chuckle. "But give it more thought, Rachel. There's a lot to be said about home and hearth and husband and baby. And the child really ought to have a father when he's grown a little."

"Great," Rachel had returned. "When the time comes, I'll buy him one." Another shudder raced up her spine. I'm doing what you told me to, Dad, she whispered. Only her lips moved. I'm going to continue the Hammond line. Isn't that what you wanted? I'll select a man all carefully designed, and if the baby looks like a Hammond it'll be a surprise. This child will be perfect. Isn't that what you wanted from your worthless daughter?

"Crying?" her doctor had asked.

Hammonds didn't cry. But all the rest of them had been hard-driven men.

"Me? Crying? Hammonds don't cry." Rachel had brushed at her eyelid. There *was* a tear there. "All the rest of that talk is sheer garbage, Sue. Listen, when you get it down to one, send him over to me for an interview.

But make damn sure he hasn't a clue about what I really want!''

And that, Rachel told herself now as she splashed a little cold water on her nervous wrists, had all been accomplished, and today was the day the winner came!

She went back to her desk, sat, stood up again, paced the room, craned her neck trying to see something—anything—from the window, and then jumped when the buzzer rang. Oh, God, what am I doing? she almost screamed at herself. Am I doing what my father wanted so badly? He wanted a son. And since I obviously didn't qualify, it's up to me to make up the shortage. She covered her ears, trembling. She could still hear her father's hoarse voice plaguing her. "I need a boy, Rachel. And quickly! A girl isn't good enough!" She moved over to the desk and sat down. Her father's chair, that. A comfortable, overstuffed swivel chair mounted on a six-inch-high platform, so that all of her visitors would have to look up at her. Lesson sixteen in her father's lexicon. "Catch them at the door and make them sweat!" To complete the scene she swiveled around so that her back was to the door.

The door opened with a squeak; there was the sound of movement behind her, and then a rush of feet. "We got him, Ms. Hammond," somebody yelled. Rachel whirled her chair around. Things were very much out of control. A chunky, husky man with white-streaked hair was standing in the doorway, one of his big hands on the throat of each of her two remaining security men. "We got him," one of the two repeated weakly.

"Yes, I can see you've got him." Sarcasm dripped all over the floor. "Cut it *out*!"

All three of them quit the ruckus on cue. "Now, what's going on?"

"I'm——" the very big stranger started to say, but she interrupted.

"I *know* who you are. What I don't know is what's going on."

"This is the guy," Leo Gurstner insisted. "I seen him out the front door. Fritz and Habblemeyer walked over across the street to see what he was doin', and he dumped them both. Both at the same time, mind you! You want I should call the cops?"

"I want," she said, sighing, "that you both would go far away and let me talk to this—gentleman. He has an appointment with me."

I have? Charlie Mathers shrugged his shoulders and rearranged his torn shirt. Well, perhaps I do. Uncle's letter was short on specifics but long on "wants."

I want you to get your butt up here and help me straighten out this girl. Do anything necessary. I can see the vultures circling around her head already.

Only his uncle was more old-fashioned than that. Butt was the polite word, which the old man would never use.

The two guards hesitated for a moment, then ducked out of the office and closed the door gently behind them. The woman was looking at him as if he were a side of beef. "And how did all *that* happen?"

Charlie shrugged his shoulders again. She had a nice voice. Deep for a woman, and marvelous control. "I was standing across the street waiting to meet you when these two yahoos came running at me. And then they both tripped over each other. One of them grabbed my shirt to keep from falling. Never saw such a thing in my whole life. I knew they came out of this building, so I thought it might be neighborly to come and tell you all about it."

"Very appropriate," Rachel said as she pursed her lips and went back to her executive chair. He was coming to see her. The game had started. Her control was instantly renewed. Perhaps her father *was* still haunting that chair. Damn. She shifted her position nervously. The big man sauntered across the room, moved the two straight-backed chairs off to one side, and pulled the couch from under the window over to take their place. Then, without a by-your-leave, he slumped into it, with one foot dangling over the end.

And now, Rachel told herself, I take control of the situation by—by how? Rack her brain as she might, she couldn't think of a sensible thing to say. So she stared. As he did.

"And what do I call you?" she finally blurted out.

"Charlie," he said softly. "Leastwise that's what my pa called me. Don't tell me that you're——"

"I'm Hammond. Now, what did the doctor tell you about me or this job?"

"Not a blessed thing," Charlie told her in all honesty. "Not a thing."

"But you can't help wondering, I suppose?"

"You could say that."

"Well, I'll tell you all about it," she said. "But first you and I have to get to know each other a great deal better than we do now. So for that purpose we'll go out to my ranch and spend a month just making ourselves acquainted. You are free to travel, I suppose?"

The big man waved a casual hand.

"And you have better clothing?"

He looked down at himself, and then up at her in chagrin. "This stuff looked pretty good when I left the hotel this morning," he said mildly. "I never expected a bunch of goons to try to tear my clothes off."

"Don't worry about that," she told him as she got up briskly, reached for the briefcase she normally took home with her, and then rejected it. No extra work, she told herself as she pressed the button on her intercom.

"Beth. I'm going out to the ranch. I'll be gone for a minimum of four weeks, and I want no interruptions while I'm out there. Absolutely none!"

"Yes, ma'am," the intercom burped. "But there's this man in the outer office who keeps trying to tell me he has an appointment with you."

"Well, call Security and have them bounce him," Rachel snapped. "I don't have any other appointments!" Rachel thumbed the switch off. For the first time in four years, Hammond Enterprises would function with nobody at the helm. "Come on—er—Charlie." She beckoned with her imperial little finger. It wasn't until moments later, locked into her private elevator with him, that she recalled how gracefully he had come to his feet and followed. It was a good beginning, she told herself. A big, healthy man, smoothly functional—and mannerly, she added as he helped her into the limousine.

"It will take some time to drive out to the Bar Nine," she told him.

"Don't mind me." He was already at the window. "I like to look at the scenery."

"That's not exactly what I had in mind," she countered. "There are a million things I want to know about you. This dossier was compiled in a hurry, so naturally there are a few things missing. Now then—you were born in...?"

"Waco, Texas," he replied. "Thirty-four years ago. Is that the kind of thing you want to know?"

"Approximately. Any communicable diseases?"

"Not now." He gave her another one of those quizzically gentle looks. "Oh, you mean childhood diseases? I guess I had everything most kids have."

"I see. And none of them—er—impaired any of your—physical functions?"

"Only one I know of is when the bull stepped on my foot," he said, nodding sagely. "On occasion when it rains the damn thing aches a little. But the Air Force doctors said there was nothin' wrong with the foot. Psycho something, they said."

"Psychosomatic?"

"The very word," he acknowledged. "Besides, it doesn't rain all that much up here in Kansas, I hear. If you're worried about experience, I ran a good-size spread by the time I was fourteen. Horses, cattle—even——" a little tinge of contempt slipped in "—sheep."

"Yes, that relieves my mind," Rachel said and, for the life of her, despite all the lists she had made beforehand, she couldn't think of a single other question to ask. For the rest of the ride she alternated, staring out of the window, and, when he did the same, shifting to stare at him.

What in the world am I doing? Rachel pondered. I could get all this information from behind a desk, on a personnel form. And that's not what I want to know. So how do you go about asking a man a question like the one I want to ask, when I can't even phrase it to myself?

Besides, he's not exactly what I expected. There's something free and easy behind all that—muscle. When he smiled he looked downright handsome. When he had something to say he seemed to think it over before wagging his tongue. But of course, as her father had warned her a time or two in her young life, "There's more handsome men sittin' on death row over in

Leavenworth than you'll find singing in any church choir!'' So she leaned back against the cushions, shut down her mind and, because she seldom got more than five hours sleep a night, promptly dropped off.

Charlie Mathers watched out of the corner of his eye as the girl swayed slightly, slumped, and snapped herself back up again. He was without a night or two of sleep himself, but long training had made it easier for him to adjust. He slid over carefully in her direction, and the next time she slumped her head landed on his shoulder and stayed there.

He shrugged himself into the most comfortable position he could find, and slipped one arm around her shoulders to keep her from bouncing away from him. Her mind might be tough, he told himself, but her shoulder is a tender morsel indeed. "Harridan." Who said that, me? It just goes to prove something or other. A lovely creature, no doubt about it, living on nerves and coffee, I suppose. I wonder what she'd be like totally relaxed? And I wonder what kind of a game I've fallen in to? Soft shoulders under his hand, soft, rounded hip pressed against his own, a narrow waist, and pert, proud breasts that bounced, unfettered, under that silk blouse. The car moved off the paved highway on to an unpaved ranch road. Charlie licked his lips appreciatively, and settled back to see what the future might bring. "Do anything you can," Uncle Roger had written, and suddenly doing just that had pleasant overtones. He licked his dry lips and settled back against the upholstery.

The famous Flat Plains of Kansas were not all that flat. Along the eastern border of the state, where the Missouri River chased itself in yellow flood, there were more than enough hills to make a decent-size mountain. A few miles to the west, in the neighborhood of

Manhattan, Topeka, Cottonwood Falls, the land looked like a child's landscape puzzle, piled up on itself. The limousine was taking them on a southwesterly line away from the town of Libertyville, up on to the rolling hills and prairie land known as the Flint Hills.

But the road went on—and on. Until finally the limousine broke out of the bottoms, across a line of sheltering trees into a little watered valley on the other side of the ridge, and rattled over a cattle guard. The weathered sign said "Bar Nine." A few head of well-fed cattle lifted their eyes briefly as the car plugged on by them. Herefords, he judged, and, penned in the far corral, what looked to be a few head of Texas Longhorns. And then they were at the ranch house, a native stone building that seemed as old as the Oregon Trail, where they had started. The car came to a halt, the girl woke up in his arms, startled, and a pair of hound dogs came baying down the wind from around the corner of the barn.

"Excuse me," she said hesitantly as she moved as far away from him as she could get.

"No excuse necessary." He grinned. It was his first tactical mistake.

Her jaw hardened. "Let's be sure there's no further need for such," she snapped.

His deep blue eyes assessed her, and decided. "Yes, ma'am," he acknowledged.

"And don't call me ma'am," she snapped. "My name is Hammond."

"I see," he said gravely. "It's just, where I come from, it isn't considered polite to call a woman by her last name without a name or title to go with it."

The first sign of rebellion, Rachel told herself. If I were in my right mind I'd fire him here and now and let him walk back. But I want more than a day's work from this man; it would pay to be a little conciliatory, just this once.

"All right," she conceded. "You may call me Rachel. Now, what's your last name?"

He seemed about to answer. At least, his mouth began to form words, but by that time the chauffeur had opened the back door of the limousine, and the hounds were on them. One of them was a middle-aged bitch who sat quietly beside the door and wiggled and whined. The other was a dog, barely a year old, exuberant, anxious. "Get down, Blue," Rachel commanded as the dog squeezed into the car and began to slobber over her. But she said it with affection.

And that, Charlie told himself, is the first time I've heard her sounding pleased about something. He squeezed out of the car, not an easy feat for a man his size. The elderly bitch looked up and inspected him carefully, then offered a triple tail wag.

"Henrietta approves of you," Rachel said. "That's in your favor. A good judge of people, is Henrietta."

"I'm glad somebody likes me," he replied as he stooped to pat the animal. Henrietta growled. "I see," he said, laughing. "Wag, but not touch, Henrietta? Don't you think that's a halfhearted commitment?" The woman behind him was startled for a moment, then controlled her face.

"We'll go up to the house," she said, indicating the broad wooden steps that led up to the porch.

"The place looks empty," he commented as he walked up the stairs behind her.

"It is, Charlie——" she said, leaving a space for him to volunteer his last name. He ignored her offer. Rachel was caught off guard again, and a tiny blush swept over her cheeks. She brushed him aside, and led the way into the house.

The front door opened directly into the small living room. She felt the need to defend herself and her possessions. "It gets cold in Kansas in the wintertime. That's why we have small rooms and low ceilings. If you would sit down on the couch, Charles?" It wasn't exactly a request, but rather the polite expression of an order that she intended he should obey. He paused to look around the room. She stood there, fuming, as he did so.

An old fireplace was blocked up, and a Ben Franklin stove stood in its recess. The wallpaper was clean, but oh, so very dull. The furniture was in good shape, but old. Grand Rapids, turn of the century, his roving eye told him. And the carpet on the floor had seen too many boots stalk across it for its own good. It might have once been burnt amber. On the wall across from the stove hung a painting of a fierce old man. "Your father, Rachel?"

"Grandfather," she replied. "My father thought that paintings were a waste of time and money. Please sit." She indicated the couch. He chose the adjacent Morris chair and sank into it with a comfortable sigh.

"There's never been a more comfortable chair than a Morris," he commented as his big hands patted the worn wooden arms. And all the while his eyes had been studying her. There was no doubt in his mind that tension was building within her, that she had kept something of extreme importance to herself that she wanted to tell him, and that she was not the type of woman to stand for delays. So he changed his tactics—for the moment. "I take it you want to tell me something?"

The air came out of her lungs in an explosive gasp as she collapsed on to the couch and tucked her skirts in.

"Yes. This month in front of us is to be a sort of test run, an opportunity for you and me to get to know each other better. There are other people on the ranch, but they will stay out of our way. Mrs. Colchester will come over every afternoon and fix us supper. There are a few head of cattle around the area, and perhaps enough outside work on the spread to keep us busy, but that's not terribly important to the test. Except for Mrs. Colchester, we will have to make do for ourselves."

"This is a test? Which one of us, do you suppose, is being tested?"

Her fleeting blush was back again, for longer than before. "That remains to be seen, doesn't it?"

"And that's all I'm to be told about it?"

"Oh, no," Rachel said coolly. "There is one more item. If the test is successful, and you comply with all the terms, you will be paid a thousand dollars a week. I imagine that a month will be enough to complete the—er—tests."

And that, Charlie Mathers told himself, is enough of all this stalling around. He pushed himself up out of the Morris chair and strolled over in front of her. "I think I could save you two or three weeks of your valuable time, and maybe a couple of thousand dollars," he offered as he pulled her up off the sofa.

"What——?"

"I have this theory," he told her. "When two people want to get close to each other, they really have to get *close*. No amount of talking will help. Close—like this." Her hands were resting in his as she glared at him. He offered her another one of those vacuous smiles, then tugged her closer. Her breasts served as a capable bumper. She almost bounced off his chest, but his hands were on her shoulders before she could slip away from him. "And then, like this," he said softly.

Rachel whimpered as his head bent over her, blocking out the light from the windows. One of his hands moved to the small of her back, bringing her tightly into his web. His mouth moved gently down on hers, brushed against her lips, and then fled upward to the lobe of her ear. She managed a breath, and a phrase. "Don't——" she started to say, and then his lips were back on hers, sealing off her mouth in a heady attack that registered shock, amazement, fear.

Charlie could feel her fear, read the shock. He lightened the pressure against her mouth. "It's all right," he murmured in her ear. "It's all right. Relax, you could get to like it." And then he sealed her mouth again with his own. Rachel felt the first returning shock, but from then onward she *experienced* the wild, roiling flashes of excitement that shot up and down her spine, blinded her to everything else, left her hanging in his arms because her own knees refused to function.

He moved her slightly away from his steel frame. She sobbed for breath. Only his arms supported her. "See," he murmured again. "That's all there is to it." Gently, as if she were a china doll, he deposited her back on the couch, where she slipped sideways, still struggling for breath.

"Now I'm sure we've saved at least a thousand dollars," he observed gently. "Care to make it two?"

"No," she whispered, and then shouted, "No! Damn you, no!"

"Okay, okay." He spread his placating hands out in front of her. "Don't take it too hard, Rachel. It was only an experiment, nothing more. If you liked it we

could try it again some day. If not, just say the word
and I'll be off back to the city."

"I—no," she stammered.

"No what? No city? No more kisses?"

"Just no," she said, and then staggered to her feet.
Another one of her father's platitudes: To dominate
people you have to be standing toe to toe with them!

But when she came that close she was trembling. She
balled her fingers up into fists, but left them hanging at
her side. It was only a kiss, she told herself fiercely.
Plenty of women get kissed in all sorts of ways. All I
have to do is settle down. Count to ten. Get the breathing
settled, and then tell him off. Or do I want to do that?
If this is the best man to be winnowed out of the field,
I don't really want to lose him. After all, it certainly
can't take long for me to get what I want from this—
giant—and then I can write him off to expenses and
forget about him! Two more breaths. She was so close
that her breasts were rubbing gently across that steel chest
of his. She blushed and put more space between them.

"I realize, Charlie, that you are—sort of—in the dark
about what's going on. And I won't be surprised to learn
that in Texas your sort of—enticement—might work very
well."

He had both hands in his pockets, his head slightly
cocked to the left, and a wide grin on his face. But there's
more than that, Rachel told herself. Look at those eyes.
Deep, dark blue. Behind his face there was a calculation
going on, as if his mind were a computer. How in the
world did *this* man get by her screening process? She
coughed a couple of times to hide her embarrassment.

"But up here in Kansas we don't go on like that," she
continued quickly.

"Well, you could have fooled me," he said, chuckling. "There seem to be plenty of kids all over this part of Kansas."

"Stop that!" She tried to stamp her foot, but the rug was too thick to make a practical noise.

"I understand—Hammond." He reached over and wiped away the tiny bit of teardrop that was working at the corner of her left eye. "I really understand. It isn't that sort of test, huh?"

And that left Rachel Hammond far up the creek without a paddle. Lying was not her usual cup of tea, but how could she answer truthfully? Because that was exactly the kind of test it was to be. "Excuse me," she said, all in a rush. "I forgot the coffee. Please sit down, Mr.—Charles."

CHAPTER TWO

RACHEL HAMMOND staggered out onto the porch the next morning, rubbing her eyes. She did not normally require more than a few hours sleep, but her machinery wasn't working well this morning. She stretched, seeming to reach higher than she ever had before in all her life. There was an itch right in the small of her back. She tried vainly to scratch it away against the porch post, with no success.

"If you was to scratch it there any more you'd get splinters." She whirled around. Charlie Mathers looked bigger and better and more—dangerous—than he had on the previous day. And he proved the point by reaching around behind her and scratching at almost the perfect place.

"A little lower," Rachel murmured, and wiggled slightly to match the occasion. He complied. She groaned with a sort of ecstasy. Naturally, with the two of them facing each other, and his hand around behind her, pushing against her, they could not help but move close together. And, Rachel realized, I haven't dressed and this nightgown is too—— But it felt so damnably comfortable that she took one more tiny quarter step in his direction.

Life was measured in millimeters, not centimeters. Nothing else would have happened except that she felt a sudden shuddering sensation run up and down her spine. Her breasts swelled, her nipples stiffened, and the

26

millimeter that separated them was gone. "Oh, God," Rachel muttered.

He made some comment, but its meaning passed completely over her head. Her nerves tingled from scalp to toenail. He swayed slightly from side to side, adding massage to contact. "Lightning," she muttered, convinced that a storm had struck.

"What?" His hands landed on her shoulders, trying to move her another millimeter forward. But this time the contact was too much. *Or too soon*, she told herself as she backed away.

"No more itch?" She looked up at him. That silly grin was on his face as he looked down at her.

"I—no," she said. "No more itch. I—thank you for your help."

"No trouble at all," he said, chuckling. "Anything you need, you just call on me. Anything. I thought I'd go look over the stables. Like to come along?"

Her heart said yes, but her mind knew better. "No, I mean to get breakfast and get dressed. Why don't you go ahead? I might join you after a while. We could go for a ride—you *do* ride?"

"Anything with four feet," he replied. "Born and raised in a saddle, I was."

"That must have been some feat," she murmured sarcastically. "Your mother must have had considerable discomfort. Excuse me, Mr.—er—Charlie."

He tipped a salute with two fingers and grinned again as she whirled away from him and disappeared behind the screen door. Yes, Charlie, he chided himself. *Do* excuse me. "The lady doth protest too much"? He shrugged his shoulders and started toward the barn.

Inside, Rachel watched him through the interstices of the muslin curtains. Big, powerful, assured. His walk

told it all. Ordinarily she wouldn't have a man of his
type within five miles of her. Here at the center of her
dream, the ranch house was almost a cloister. Herself,
Mrs. Colchester, and the ranch hands. And now this
man? What was it about him that had caused Sue to
nominate him? He hardly matched any two of the ten
requirements she had laid down. And so? Declare him
unusable and send him packing? Or give him a long
trial—if that can be done without burning my fingers.
She closed her eyes for just a moment, and memory
crowded her. "I vote to keep him," she said, chuckling,
as she sat down to a bigger breakfast than normal.

"You've got a couple of fine quarter horses in this pair,"
Charlie told her as he led the mare out of her stall and
walked her in a circle. "Good form, nice fetlocks—her
left shoe's a mite worn on one side. Want me to saddle
up for you?"

Rachel Hammond had had enough time to restore her
perpetual grouch. She was wearing a pair of blue jeans,
the legs tucked into her boots, and a loose red blouse,
open at the neck, but contained by a blue and red
bandana. And a white ten-gallon hat, covering all her
magnificent curls. Besides, he was so damnably big. Lord
knew what he might do if angered. "Oh, so now you're
a blacksmith too?"

He grinned at her, that amiable grin that irritated her
even more than normal. "Like to keep my hand in most
anything," he said, and then he had the colossal nerve
to look her up and down as if she were a prime heifer.
"Saddle up?"

Rachel would have loved to reject his offer.
Unfortunately, her working Western saddle was heavy.
There was always a borderline between getting revenge

and getting a hernia, she told herself. One of her dad's old sayings. God, how I worshiped that man, and for what?

"Saddle up," she mumbled, and turned away so that he could not read her face.

He was a quick worker. He hummed as he worked. One good item, one bad. Having no ear for music herself, she hated to hear other people enjoying themselves with song. She tucked up her hair under her riding cap, brushed by him, and mounted, all with an economy of motion that he could not help but admire. "Well, don't just stand there, cowboy."

He grinned up at her again, and swung into his own saddle as gracefully as anyone might. Another tip to the brim of his hat. "Yes, ma'am."

"I told you not to call me ma'am," she snapped at him as she turned her mare out into the farmyard.

"Yes, ma'am," he acknowledged. Fuming, Rachel admitted her defeat by refusing to repeat herself. Instead she clapped her heels against her mount's sides, and went cantering off up the hill south of the house.

The area around the house was hard-packed dirt, as with most ranch houses. But just a few yards away from that empty area, they were riding stirrup-deep in the yellow and green and red flowers that constituted true prairie grass. "Never seen anything like this back in Texas," he admitted. He pulled his high-stepping gelding to a halt and pushed his hat to the back of his head. "Ooooee. Ain't that something?"

She nodded in agreement. From horizon to horizon the land sparkled with color, and she loved it. And if this simple soul feels the same, we have *something* in common, she decided.

"There aren't many places like this left in the country," she told him. "Flint Hills here is about the biggest stretch of prairie in the West. When the first settlers came to this land it was all prairie. Mile after mile in all directions. For a time it was all ranching. Nothing could tame that tough soil. My grandfather could still remember when the prairie grass was as tall as a horse's saddle. Somewhere around 1836, somebody brought in the steel plow. It broke through the crust and Kansas became farm land. Well, not everywhere. Nowadays you'll see wheat and corn and oil wells and factory zones. And occasionally one little space of the prairie left. The name here will tell you why. Flint Hills. Even the steel plough couldn't break through this rocky land. But the prairie grasses can—and do."

"And here I rode all this distance expecting to find the tall corn growing," he said mournfully. "And look, there's not a tree in sight."

How it's possible for a big man to look so downtrodden I'll never know, Rachel told herself. He has such a mobile face. Sometimes I wonder if it's all a put-on?

"More likely wheat and manufacturing—and the Army," she said. "And tornadoes and prairie grass. Trees spell the death of a prairie. It destroys the ambience of the soil. Ride out west of here. You'll see trees phasing in, and the gradual ending of the prairie. It's a delicate balance."

He reined his mount in and stepped down from the saddle. She watched as he kicked at the dirt. His horse pawed, and there was a little spark of fire where the iron-shod foot scraped over the hard flint.

"And that," she told him, "is why this little patch of ground was never plowed under. About as scrawny and scratchy a piece of land as you ever did see. But the prairie grass grows here, mainly because the roots go straight down for a considerable distance. And as long as we don't over graze the area, all this will survive. Come on, Mr. Texan, let's see what you can do."

She rode without spurs. As soon as her heels touched the mare, the beast was off like a shot of lightning. His own gelding pranced for a moment, adding another second or two of delay before he could tuck his boot into the stirrup and swing aboard. And then, to make things worse, his mount began to move out after the mare before Charlie could get himself fully settled.

"Maybe it isn't the woman I'd better watch out for," he muttered as he fumbled for his other stirrup. But once in the saddle his much bigger animal proved its worth. Within five minutes they were neck and neck, close enough to touch, until an ancient pinnacle of flint separated them. He came around the far side of the pinnacle, racing for all he was worth. Just out of the corner of his eye he noticed that Rachel had reined in her mount, and her mare dug in her heels and wheeled to a stop.

He was still racing and whooping, feeling like a fool as her mare performed in the old tradition, "Turn on a dime and give you five cents change." By the time he could wrestle the gelding to a stop and turn him around, the woman had dismounted. When he came up to her, Rachel Hammond was thin-lipped as she tried to keep from laughing.

He drew up beside her, solemn-faced. She let a giggle escape. Still no reaction. "Isn't there anything that'll make you mad?" she asked.

"Nothing recently," he drawled as he swung down and ground-reined his mount. "Of course, there's no telling. What's that old saying? 'You fool me once, shame on you. You fool me twice, shame on me!'"

Although he was still smiling, Rachel could feel the
cold radiating from him. Cold steel, she told herself.
Watch out, girl. This is not a man to be crossed! Still,
she could not hold back.

"Now, I think we'll go down to the corral," she announced, "and you can show me how good you are at
roping one of those steers."

He walked over and confronted her, barely an inch
away. "You mean one of those longhorns?"

"Why, of course." She slapped the dust off her jeans,
using her hat as a fan. The mare snorted, and did a
stutter-step, but the girl controlled her with ease, and
swung aboard.

"You want me to rope one of them steers, single-
handed? Inside that tiny corral?"

"Why, yes. And hog tie it. You aren't scared, are
you?"

"I'm not a rodeo rider," he told her softly. "And
you're darn well right I'm scared," he told her as he
swung back up on to his mount. "Only a fool would
take a chance like that. And my pappy never raised any
fools—ma'am. Out in the open with a lot of running
room, where the other cattle could spread, that would
be a different thing. But penned up in there with all those
longhorns? No, thankee, ma'am."

He was off before Rachel could muster up another
word. And when she *did* find the word, it was the sort
that her mother would have paddled her for! So she said
it again, and trailed back to the ranch.

They met for dinner that night. She was pacing the living
room. Take her miles away from Libertyville, he told
himself, and she's beginning to change a bit. Her hair
was up in a classic chignon, her body masked by the

masculine double-breasted suit. But there was a softness about her. Her face was no longer masked by that impenetrable look of command. Even without makeup there was a subtle femininity. There were differences between her and the picture of her grandfather hanging on the wall. *But* she's no longer a unisex businessperson, Charlie thought as he wandered into the room. She was standing by the closed-off fireplace, a martini in one hand.

"You're ten minutes late." She confirmed by looking down at her wristwatch, then took a sip of her drink.

"You said eight-thirty," he replied as he tugged at a gold chain that led to his shirt pocket. She glared as he hoisted out a massive gold watch and flipped its cover open. "Eight thirty-five," he commented. "By golly, I *am* late. Five minutes late!"

"Ten minutes," she said, using her most frigid tone. Just at that minute, the big grandfather clock in the hall struck the half hour.

"We're both wrong," he said, chuckling. "It's only eight-thirty. Which means I'm not late at all." He rushed across the room and began to pat her on the back. She had been taking another sip of the cocktail when he came out with that ridiculous statement, *We're both wrong!* Somehow the liquid got down the wrong pipe, and Rachel was choking.

He whipped her around in front of him, her back hard against his massive chest. His hands joined in front of her, knuckles in, just at her solar plexus. With one massive heave he forced the alcohol back up, and cleared her breathing tube. Unfortunately, since alcohol was a liquid, it sprayed out through her half-opened mouth and soaked the love seat in front of her.

Rachel gasped, but managed to refill her lungs—and her temper as well. "Now look what you've done," she raged.

"Better wet the furniture than let you choke to death, lady."

"That's a very valuable piece of furniture." She wanted to shout at him, but had not enough breath left.

"Is that so?" he drawled. "Looks like Grand Rapids, 1900."

Rachel forced herself to settle down. It took some doing. And, while she did her deep-breathing exercises, she thought. When he's right, he's right. He just saved my life by applying the Heimlich maneuver. And then I complained because he made me spit up over a relatively useless chair. I owe him an apology.

Apologies were a thing that Rachel Hammond had long since discarded. But she could not just stand there, blinking her eyes at him. "Grand Rapids, 1897," she said. "Would you like a drink?"

He grinned at her. He knows, she told herself nervously. He understands what's going on. Dear Lord, what have I done? Chosen a man who's too smart for me?

"I could use a shot of red-eye," he suggested. "Seems to me it's been mighty cold in these parts all night long."

"Red-eye?"

"Rye whiskey."

"What sort of mix?"

"Nothing," he said, and that grin—that infernal grin—was back again. "My pappy told me that the only way to avoid getting drunk was to stick to one choice and drink it straight."

"Your pappy seemed to have a lot to say," she returned, gesturing him to a chair. "Now. Tell me something about yourself, Mr.—Charlie. Something real, for a change. Your pappy?"

"Not like me," he started out. "My pappy died young. In the wars, you know. Now my grandpappy is a *big* man. Spent a part of his life as a sky pilot, and then switched full-time to ranching."

"Sky pilot?" she said sarcastically. "You're beginning to sound like a very poorly written Western novel. So your grandfather was a preacher?"

"The best, lady. Still is. Got him a deep, strong voice. When he says 'hell fire' you just know that if you look around you the flames is coming straight at you. Evangelical. Preaches the old-time religion. Hell fire and damnation! In these parts, too."

"You mean he had a parish in this neighborhood?"

"Well, not exactly. Gramps was a chaplain in the Army. Served over here at Fort Riley, then up at Fort Leavenworth. When he retired from the Army he went off back to Texas, and the family spread down there. A hard, God-fearing man. Yes, ma'am."

Mrs. Colchester came into the room, her face flushed, her white head bobbing back and forth like a pigeon on the strut. "Dinner," she said. Charlie pulled himself to his feet and offered Rachel his arm. She shrugged it off.

"We don't bother with that sort of nonsense," she said, and floated by him and out of the door. Notice that, he told himself. Floated. It almost seemed to be. A longer skirt—the 1890 model, where her legs were invisible—and she'd look like a Navy destroyer, steaming up to dock! On the other hand, any man who would do anything to hide those magnificent legs of her ought to have his head examined! He came into the dining room with a wry grin on his face.

"Something's funny?" She might have done away with *some* of the old customs, but she was standing there beside the chair at the head of the table, waiting for him to pull it out and seat her. He moved around Mrs. Colchester to do just that.

"Funny? No, something pleasant, ma'am." He pulled her chair out and waited while she seated herself.

"And don't call me ma'am," she said. She glowered up at him. Her lips were already formed to say the same thing.

"You'll have to excuse me. I'm trying, but it's a hard thing to forget. My apologies."

All the food was already on the table. There'll be no fancy serving in this house, he thought as he lifted the platter of steaks and offered her a choice.

"I can reach everything on the table," she snapped. She sounded like some ambitious lieutenant on his first night in the field mess, and for a moment former Colonel Charlie Mathers felt like chewing her up one side and down the other, but decided on a twinkle instead. He set the platter down near her plate.

"And now what are you grinning at?"

"Nothing, ma'am—I mean, nothing. This all reminded me of a play I once saw."

"A play? You saw a play?"

"Well, I didn't spend *all* my time chasing the north end of a cow headed south," he drawled. "I believe the author was Shakespeare. Or something of that nature. I *did* go to school," he mused. "Right nice it was in those days."

"Don't tell me. Texas Agricultural?"

"Now that's a nice school too," he agreed. "But I didn't go there. I went to Southern Methodist. One of those little religious schools. My Gramps being a preacher and all——"

"Yes, yes, I understand." She was eating with both hands, industriously. Steak and potatoes and greens.

And there's another thing I could do, he told himself. Get her out of the stable and into the living room. Eventually they arrived at the coffee.

"What do you think about children?" She threw it in his face to watch the reaction. There didn't seem to be much of a change.

"Children," he mused. "Well, I can take them or leave them. That is if we're talking about *other* people's kids. Now my own—well, that's a different matter."

She jumped on the phrase. "You have children?"

"Not that I know of. On one or two occasions I thought—but, well, it was a minor mistake. You know how that is."

"No, I don't know. Tell me."

"Somehow it seems to me that there's a conversation going on beneath a conversation. If you want to know something specific, why don't you just come out and ask it? Or maybe give me a chance to ask a question or two?"

"All right. If you want to know something, go ahead and ask." And if it isn't too far off base, she thought, I might even answer it. What in the world is the matter with me? I'm going all soft inside. If Grampa could have seen this performance, he'd have got a big stick and beat me something terrible! "But Mrs. Colchester will want to clear the table right now. Why don't we go out on the veranda and talk?"

It was not an invitation, he noted. It was a command. He smiled, helped her with her chair, and followed her outside, to where a broad veranda circled three sides of the old stone house. A couple of lounge chairs were already grouped around a small table, and a steaming pot of coffee sat in the middle of the table.

"Now, then?"

"First of all, what the devil connection is there between all this——" he waved his hand outward to the stomping of the cattle in their pen, the sound of night birds closing in on them, the smell of the flowers in the prairie grass "—and that muck-raking magazine down town? Which, I am told, you run with considerable enjoyment?"

Her face flushed for a moment. She sipped a little coffee to help control her impulse to anger. "Money," she said. "My grandfather left me this ranch to save or kill. My father left me the magazine. The magazine makes money. The ranch doesn't. I wish it were the other way around, but it isn't."

"So you plow all your profits into the ranch?"

"Not exactly," she retorted. "I don't own all this out-right. There are other stockholders. All of whom groan and complain every year when I tell them how much money the ranch is losing." She looked at him over the rim of her coffee mug. Her eyes were sparking. "And don't, for heaven's sake, ask me, 'What's a nice girl like you doing in a place like this?'"

"Oh, I wouldn't ask a fool question like that. I already know the answer. You're just not a nice girl."

Her mug trembled in her hand, and almost fell to the floor. Got you with that one, didn't I? he thought. The dear little girl wants to appear to be a shrew, but doesn't want to be called one! Step one; now let's move on.

"It seems to me, ma'am," he said, "that you're going at this the wrong way around. It's the ranch that's losing money, not the magazine. Why don't you hire some

smart hombre to run the ranch, cut down on a few of
the sore spots, and make the ranch run a profit? It *must*
be possible. Aren't there four or five other big spreads
in the area? Some of them must be making a profit.''

"Seven, to be exact," she snapped. She set her mug
down on the table with considerable emphasis. "I
suppose you think you could take things in hand
yourself?"

"Well now, I may not be the best cowpoke ever came
down the pike, but I can see one or two little things that
might be worthwhile."

Cold seemed to settle between them. Not an arctic cold
wave from the North Pole, such as winter might bring,
but an emotional cold. Rachel Hammond had disappeared; Hammond the executive had taken her place.
"Give me a sample or two," she commanded.

"Easy enough," he drawled. "Oh, if you don't mind,
ma'am, I don't smoke, and I don't like to be around
people who do."

Rachel, who had a cigarette halfway to her mouth,
paused. Her ordinary reaction would be to light a fire
under the man, which would send him running straight
back to Texas. "But just for the hell of it," her little
devils whispered to her, and she killed the flame and
dropped the butt into the nearby ashtray.

"You think that's important, do you?" Another
struggle was going on beneath the surface, he could see.
Her fists were clenched.

"Yes. Have you ever tried kissing a girl who's been
smoking? Tastes like you were licking an old, greasy rag.
Now, I was about to say——"

"I can't say that I've made a habit of kissing girls who
smoke," she interrupted. "And before you go any

further, Charlie, I've read Shakespeare myself. *The Taming of the Shrew*, wasn't it?''

He watched her, curious to see what other responses might erupt. When none followed, he went back to his story. "Take those longhorns," he said. "There's a big speciality market for lean meat these days. But you can't raise enough beef to satisfy the market by keeping them penned in. You need to let them run the range.''

"Sure I do," she muttered. "Only then I need to keep them from interbreeding with my Herefords, and I have to put more men riding fence lines and watching, otherwise those longhorns will raise the devil with everything else that walks.''

"Not if you take the time to de-horn them," he said. "Ain't no big problem. De-horn them, put your brand on them, and turn them loose. How many men have you got riding for the brand right now?''

"Two," she said, sighing. "It's all I can afford.''

"You have to spend money to make money," he said. "One or two cowpokes could do the work, providing you had a helicopter to do it with.''

"Helicopter! I'm barely keeping my head above water, and now you want me to trade an inexpensive cowpoke for an expensive helicopter pilot? You're crazy, man. Crazy!''

He stood, stretching, and looked down at her. The moon was up, a three-quarter silver dollar, and its soft rays had erased all of her worry lines, all of her sternness. Very suddenly, Rachel Hammond looked like a frightened little girl. And Uncle Roger wanted me to come up to Kansas, he reminded himself, because he feared something would happen, or was happening, to this last of the Hammond family. What?

"Chopper pilots." He half turned away from her. "The woods are full of chopper pilots. All those thousands we've trained for Vietnam, for the Persian Gulf. They're all around you, lady, looking for a chance to make a buck."

"And how do you know that?"

"Because I'm one of them myself, ma'am. And I'll bet that I could scratch up half a dozen more. Good cattlemen, who also can fly a chopper. What say, Ms. Hammond?"

She struggled to her feet, with his hand helping, biting her lower lip. "Just who are you?" she asked softly. "What the devil is going on around here? I didn't hire you to be a cowpoke—and yet you are one. I don't need a ranch foreman—and yet you talk like one. I didn't want a helicopter pilot—what else are you?"

"Just an ordinary man looking for work," he said. He spoke as softly as she, so she moved closer.

"I wish I could believe that."

"Believe it," he answered. "What you see is what you get. And if you didn't hire me for any of those particulars, just what the devil *did* you hire me for? Or, come to think of it, did you hire me at all?"

Rachel felt something in the pit of her stomach. Not exactly a pain, but rather a disturbance. Brought on either by this man or the things he talked about. Was there really something she could do to make the ranch profitable? Would it be possible to make over the *Gossiper* into something more to her liking? And what effect would any of that have on her primary goal?

Without realizing it, she found his arm around her shoulder. The night winds were chilling. His warmth was just what she needed at the moment. And it was just then that her practical mind shifted into gear. She shrugged out of his grasp, settled her blouse and skirt, and cleared her throat.

"Yes, I'm hiring you," she said. Charlie could feel the change. Hammond was back with him; Lord knew where Rachel had disappeared. "And I don't mind your taking a little interest in the ranch. After all, the primary reason for all this is for us to become acquainted."

"Why?" he asked. "Why do we go through all this just because you want us two to become acquainted?"

She moved away from him. A safe distance, her mind told her. From this point on I've got to keep the barriers up. I've got to remember that it's a business proposition I'm working at. Strictly business. Gawd, Daddy, why did you lay this on me?

"What I want," she told him, "is for you to give me a baby."

CHAPTER THREE

A MILLION raging thoughts went through Rachel's mind as she watched Charlie's broad back disappear into the evening darkness. If I had the strength, she assured herself, I would go after him and hit him over the head with—whatever I could find on the way! But I don't have it—the strength, that is. How dare he turn his back on me?

And not a word about her statement. It had taken her the whole day to decide exactly how she planned to say it to him. And when he heard the sentence he had stood quietly in front of her, his lips had pursed in and out a time or two, and then, without saying a word, neither yea or nay, he had solemnly tipped her a salute and stalked away. The nerve of the man!

Only then, as she leaned against the pillar that held up the porch roof, did she begin to doubt herself. Did I say it wrong? she asked herself. Too explicit. Not explicit enough? Or does he expect something more than a straightforward business proposition? She leaned against the post. Whatever he planned to do, it would be done out of sight. Suddenly all her memories crowded in on her, and they hurt.

Her father was a disciplinarian of the worst sort. He had driven his only son to drink and death, and then tried to convert shy little Rachel into a replacement. It had been a soul-piercing conversion, ending up with the stone-faced Hammond of *Gossiper* fame. Only on the most difficult occasions, and then only in private, had

43

Rachel come out from behind her Hammond disguise
to cry.

This was one of those occasions. Mrs. Colchester had
left to go back to her own cottage. And Charlie whatever-
his-name-was had stalked off into the night. Weary,
feeling twice her real age, Rachel stumbled down the
hall in the semidarkness, fumbled with her door, and
threw herself on her bed.

The tears finally ended. She gathered herself up. No
mere man was going to control her. There had to be a
way around this initial setback. What was it?

She flipped on the overhead light. No mollycoddling
lamps for Hammond. Only a bare bulb in a ceiling
fixture, just the way her father had always prescribed.
With the light on, she was facing herself in the full-length
mirror behind the door. And another startling thought.
One which she had never thought before. Not in all her
life. Am I not—good-looking enough?

I thought that men were ready to—do that at the drop
of a hat. In fact, from her readings she had come to
believe that not even an invitation was needed! And besides, that wasn't the way she meant to have it
accomplished!

Warily she scanned her reflection. No, not beauty. A
mannish look would be desirable; instead she looked like
a Dresden doll. Not at all satisfactory. The blond curly
hair looked almost artificial in the bright white light from
the ceiling. Her face was round, with pearly skin. A little
too perfect. And blue eyes, tear-swollen eyes. Slowly she
slipped off the rest of her clothes and studied the reflection. Her breasts bothered her the most. Her father
had required that any feminine appearance be sup-
pressed. Over the years, as she developed normally,
everything appeared abnormal. In the last year of her

father's life she had taken to binding her breasts. And now, as she was standing nude and alone, their size and shape could not be accepted.

Her narrow waist was no help at all. It pinched her in, and then swelled out into hips that seemed ... Disgusted, she turned away from the mirror, slipped into her simple cotton nightgown, and pushed the light switch.

The electricity went off on command, but the moon was something else again. It poured through her two bedroom windows, and refused to go away. Although she savored the summer night's breeze, she forced herself to pull the drapes, and then felt her way across the darkened room and fell into her narrow bed.

Not to sleep. Sleep was something that came after days of overwork. Then one took two sleeping pills, hurried into bed, and was eventually slugged into unconsciousness. But she hadn't worn herself down physically on this day, and she hated the thought of the pills. So she struggled and tossed and turned throughout the night. Nightmares raged through her mind. Black and white dreams of all the worst things her mind could conceive. Not until the rooster over in the chicken coop began to sound off, an hour or more before dawn, was she able to fall asleep.

Charlie Mathers was not a man who had trouble with sleeping. He worked or played all the hours God sent, and then fell into an easy, well-earned sleep. It was a light sleep, though. All the nights of his adult life he had slept with a secret internal alarm watching over him. He took a long walk up the hill to the corral where the longhorns had bedded down early. Now, almost at midnight, the herd leader stirred, and all the others moved at the same time. It was a sort of simple ritual, such as humans might do, rolling over in their sleep to find a more comfortable position. Far in the distance, out on the range, a coyote shrilled.

What in the world is going on? his busy mind asked. Did she say what I thought she said? In those exact words? "What I want is for you to give me a baby"? More than one woman of his acquaintance had sent him signals of that nature, but always in insinuation, never in specific words. Did she think I was going to jump on her? Slam, bang, thank you, ma'am?

This girl was one crazy, mixed-up creature. Was this what Uncle Roger had seen, the sight that caused him to write to me to hurry home? Of course, when you were serving in the Air Force, you could hardly hurry off at a moment's notice. Generals might; colonels certainly didn't. They waited until they had their retirement papers in hand before they came steaming across the oceans to home, where Uncle's letter had been waiting. Play it cool, he told himself, as he wandered back down the hill toward the house. There was a dark shape waiting for him on the front porch.

Guard dog? It hardly seemed likely, yet it was so. Old Henrietta battered the porch floor a time or two with her tail, and offered to lick his proffered hand. Lord, even the dog is waiting for me to do *something*, he told himself. And I'm the only dope on the spread who doesn't seem to know just what *something* needed to be done! Disgusted with himself, he wandered down the darkened hall, guiding himself with one hand on the wall, until eventually he found his own place, went in, and collapsed on to the bed. Where, despite all the niggling, he promptly fell asleep, and made not a move until the cock crowed at dawn, Kansas time.

*　　*　　*

"Got my share of it," Charlie said, and offered his
most vacuous grin for their approval.

"Hot damn," the foreman said through clenched
th. "A curious pilgrim. Where are you from, boy?"

'Texas. Now, about those longhorns."

Ain't been any longhorns around this spread in
ty years," the forman told him. "Now why don't
ip back into the house and get about pleasing Ms.
!? I'm sure there's somethin' you could be doing
itchen. We've got man's work to do."

I'll bet you have." Charlie stepped out of the
watched the three of them saddle up and ride
minutes later he located the gelding he had
day before, and followed suit.

seemed to remember him. It whickered as
did a round dozen prancing dance steps,
ded out in the generally south direction.
ted to run; Charlie slacked off on the reins

emed to go forever over rolling, climbing
airie did, but the fence seemed to stop.
and took a better look. About fifty feet
nce was gone. Not down, but gone
hard to track individual cattle tracks
rowth. On this side of the fence, that
ide it was easy to see the tire tracks
uck that had come more than once
in the distance now, Charlie could
f auto traffic. Route 35—he knew
y over in that direction.

Charlie murmured. "It would
han one fish in the sea in these
his wristwatch. It wa-
next appointment w

Nobody appeared at the breakfast table at seven o'clock.
Mrs. Colchester shook her head. No good can come of
it, she told herself as she loaded up the plates in the
kitchen and brought them through. No good can come
of a man and a woman sharing the same house, un-
married. Her Calvinist soul screamed for her to do
something. But all she knew to do was to put the cooked
breakfast on the table and go back to her cleaning. So
she did.

When Charlie appeared at eight o'clock the eggs were
cold, the oatmeal had congealed, and the coffee looked
as if it had grown moss. But Charlie, knowing it was
his own fault, did the best he could with the eggs, ignored the oatmeal, and really enjoyed the coffee. At least
its heating pad had kept it warm, and everyone knew
how rotten the coffee could get to be in the military.

When Rachel appeared at nine o'clock, she looked
like the wrath of God had struck her. Her hair was all
pushed to one side, her robe just barely covered her
nightgown, and her eyes were filled with sleep.

"Good morning," he essayed.

"Shut up," she groaned. "Nobody talks to me before
my coffee." She fumbled over to the table and dropped
heavily into a chair. Charlie, who was feeling almost
human, poured her a mug of coffee. She surrounded the
mug with both hands, treasuring the warmth, and then
took a sip.

"Great day in the morning!" she howled. "You're
trying to poison me! Who made this slop?"

"Not me. That's the way I found it. I thought it tasted
pretty good."

Rachel carefully grounded the mug on the tabletop
and pushed her hair back off her eyes. "You?"

"Charlie," he said. "You remember? Charlie. You invited me out to spend a month on your ranch, and then——"

"Stop. Don't tell me any more. Have you eaten anything?"

"Yes. Cold eggs. Not bad, except they were fried in grease, not in butter, and they——"

"Dear Lord protect me," she muttered as she picked up a piece of burnt, cold toast. "Look, Mr.—Charles. We need to talk. But not now. Would you please go away and then join me in my office after lunch?"

"You're the boss." He scraped back his chair and made a quick exit. In the hall he ran into Mrs. Colchester. "You enjoyed your breakfast?" the housekeeper asked. Charlie took a good look at her. She didn't sound sarcastic, but then one never knew.

"Yes," he said. "The coffee was fine, but I don't care for fried eggs. And I don't see how Hammond is going to eat that oatmeal."

"Hah!" Mrs. Colchester did her best to look him straight in the eye, which was difficult because she was so short. "If you'd come at the right time, it would've been a good meal. God's punishment, that's what."

Charlie Mathers, who had spent all his formative years within the family of a parson, perked up his ears. God's punishment for coming late for breakfast? Probably something out of the Old Testament? There was a time he could spot almost any quotation from the Bible, but not any more.

"And her father would never have let her leave the table if she came in late, without eating everything in sight. A firm, sound man, her father was."

"Yes, I can see he must have been," Charlie said. He looked back through the open door into the dining room.

Rachel Hammond was hunched over, fighting to the oatmeal, her face almost screwed up into

"Spare the rod and spoil the child," the h said as she swept out of the hall.

"Yes," Charlie repeated. "I'm sure he some sort of man." Mrs. Colchester s was the first time he had seen the o evidently thought he was agreeing head, he stomped out of the hou the stables.

Much to his surprise, there One of them came stalking who the hell are you?"

Charlie looked him ov with a face much wri too old, on second l had been pounded any finishing touc he thought of foreman," he

"Yeah, I'

"Oh, I c
I guess."

"He
over.
boy

twen
you s
Rache
in the
"Yes
way and
out. A fe
ridden the
The hors
he mounted
and then he
The horse wa
and let him g
The prairie s
country. The pr
Charlie reined in
of barbed wire
completely. It was
in the high prairie g
was. On the other s
of a huge truck. A t
to the same spot. A
hear the subdued roar
the Kansas Turnpike la
"Well, now, horse,"
seem that there's more
parts." He checked with
noon. Almost time for his

jeered a

He turned his mount back toward the ranch house. The horse seemed disappointed at having its run curtailed, but after a moment he picked up speed. They both had worked up a sweat by the time they pulled up in the stable area. The lunch bell was ringing.

Charlie ducked his head in the water bucket sitting next to the horse trough, and ran for the house. He had many interesting questions he wanted to ask, and was afraid of what some of the answers might be.

Rachel Hammond had preceded him into the dining room. "About time," she said gracelessly. "You don't seem to understand. We prize promptness here. Another minute or two and you'd go hungry."

Charlie dropped into the chair at her side, rather than the place set at the far end of the table. "At least I don't have to eat cold oatmeal," he said.

She flared up immediately. Flared up, grew tense, showed color on her face, and on the parts of her neck that her dress revealed. But said not a word. She *had* dressed, Charlie noted, comparing her presence to what he had seen at breakfast. Her hair was neatly combed, the unruly curls tamed for the moment. Her utilitarian high-collar gray dress failed her purpose—to be unnoticeable. It clung lovingly to a figure that was more than adequate. Her blue eyes shot spears at him.

When she had regained her control, she said, "You try hard to be obnoxious, don't you? I'm not sure that——"

"That I'm the man you want? Maybe I could suggest a few other things I might be able to do for you."

Mrs. Colchester came in at that moment, carrying a single tray and two plates. What you see is what you get, Charlie told himself as he looked down at the tiny sandwich and the decorative pickle on the plate that was put before him.

Rachel picked up her fork and began. "You were saying?"

"I think I could suggest some ways for you to make your ranch pay," he told her. "That would give you a chance to relax from the magazine."

"Why do you think I would want to relax?" Rachel sat up straight in her chair and pulled her shoulders back. What in the world would I do with time to relax? she asked herself. Sew a fine seam? Lord, I hate sewing. Does this—man—think he can run *my* life? Her chin tilted just the slightest bit higher.

"Can't eat if you can't see the plate, lady. About the relaxing?"

"All right. What about it?"

"You have a foreman here for the ranch?"

"Of course. Mr. Hendrix. He's been here since before my father died."

"And about how often did you manage to get out here? Before this present visit, I mean."

"Are you trying to say I neglect the ranch?"

"No, nothin' like that. How often, please, ma'am?"

"I—oh, the devil with it. I make it a practice to come out here four times a year. Well, theoretically, that's my schedule. This last year we've been having trouble with the magazine. I didn't get out at the Christmas season, nor at the autumn roundup."

"Pressing business at the magazine," he commented. "Of course, if you have faith in your foreman there'd be no problem." He had to stop talking at this point. His insulted palate was trying to tell him something. Sandwich? Not beef, or ham, or make-do peanut butter. He picked up the quartered corner and did his best to inspect without actually doing so. Watercress and cucumber?

"A family tradition," she told him. "My father enjoyed it."

"I'll bet he did," Charlie murmured, and did his best to hide the look of repulsion on his face. "But for a working cowboy——"

"Yes?"

"As I said yesterday, Ms. Rachel, I've been running spreads bigger than this since I was fourteen years old, and if you would like to take advantage of my experience for as long as we're going to be here I would certainly enjoy it. A month is a long time for a man like me to have only one objective."

He knew the moment the words were out of his mouth that he had said too many of them. *Only one objective?* But the girl beside him was considering, and to his surprise she picked up a different point from that he had expected.

"You ran this spread you speak of all by yourself?"

"Of course not. Pa was busy most of the time, and Ma was helping him. But I had plenty of help. I was the oldest kid in the family, but with four brothers and three sisters——"

"That many?" He had struck an interesting point. Her eyes lit up, and her head snapped out of is customary crouch.

"Yes, ma'am. That many. We managed to rub along real well. To tell the truth, if you didn't rub along in my family all the rest would gang up on you. That was before they all got married, that is."

"*All* got married?"

"Well, all but me. After schooling, I decided to go adventuring. My brother Albert took over the home spread, and all the others found jobs in our corporation. And then they—well, my mother used to say it was an old Irish tradition. If you can't out-fight your enemy, out-populate them!''

Rachel's fork fell on to the plate with a dull clang. ''You—they all have families?''

''You'd better believe it,'' he said, chuckling. ''Our family reunions are like the mustering of the clan back in the old country. I can't remember the exact count, but I have a birthday remembrance book with three or four entries for every month. Now, how about it? Would you like me to help you around the ranch?''

For the first time that day, Rachel Hammond seemed to light up all over. ''Well, Charlie,'' she said eagerly, ''I think there are lots of things you could help me with. Now, have you finished your lunch? Is there something else you'd like?''

Charlie Mathers looked up over Rachel's head. Mrs. Colchester was standing in the doorway, a large smirk on her face. ''Yes,'' he said, ''there certainly is. I'd like a couple of hamburgers and a cup of real coffee.''

It was late that afternoon when the serene calm of the ranch was almost totally destroyed. Charlie had settled himself in the living room next to the telephone, and had made half a dozen calls in private, when he heard a horse come galloping up to the house, and a few minutes later a pair of loud voices from the office. To snoop or not to snoop had never been a problem for Charlie. One gathered as much information as one could, in whatever manner, if one intended to be a success in anything, from love to labor.

When the voices rose higher, he got up and stalked down the hall. Outside Henrietta was whining on the

porch, upset by the sound. The office door was half
open. Without a "by your leave," he walked in. Rachel
was sitting behind a huge desk, almost bouncing up and
down in the grip of some excitement. The range foreman,
Hendrix, was leaning over the desk, pounding his fist
on the mahogany finish.

"Look here," Hendrix said. "I'm the foreman. I run
this ranch. Whatever happened to those longhorns is my
business! I've been running this ranch according to all
your father's rules for almost half your lifetime. Who
put you up to this, Hammond? That imported wimp
you brought home with you?"

Rachel was in such a state that she was almost weeping.
She runs the magazine with whip in hand, Charlie told
himself, but she doesn't seem to have any control at all
over the ranch. Because she felt she had to run it the
way her father did? Lord, what a lot that man has to
account for! But this is where the changes need to begin.
He came up behind the foreman and tapped him on the
shoulder. Hendrix straightened up and turned around.
He was a tall, well-formed man, this foreman, standing
inches above Charlie's height, and perhaps twenty
pounds more in weight. But he hadn't the muscles, the
build that Charlie had. He tried to shrug off Charlie's
hand from his shoulder to no avail.

"We mustn't forget," the Texan said softly, "that it's
Ms. Rachel who's in charge around here, must we?" He
flexed his fingers. They bit into Hendrix's shoulder, and
the foreman winced. "Isn't that true?"

"I—yes, damn you! Turn me loose!"

"When I'm ready. Ms. Rachel wanted to tell you that
I'm going to be assisting you around the spread for a
few weeks. Isn't that right, ma'am?"

"Yes," Rachel agreed, as she sank back into her chair and sniffed at an incipient tear. "Yes. He's going to help!" Spoken with much more conviction, that last part.

"After thirty years around this ranch, I don't need no help from him," Hendrix roared. "Your father would never do anything like that!"

"But her father isn't with us any more." Again that soft but persistent voice from Charlie, compounded with another dig of his fingers into Hendrix's soft shoulder muscles.

"Well, I'm not going to——" Hendrix roared, and then broke off. Charlie Mathers had transferred his one hand from the shoulder muscles to the lapels of the bigger man's shirt, and had picked him up an inch or two off the floor.

"Before somebody says something that he might regret, why don't you and I walk out on the veranda for a private conversation?" The foreman hardly had the capacity to rebel. His feet paddled as he was towed out of the door. Charlie winked at Rachel as he stepped out of the room. The girl sank back again in her padded chair, and sighed.

"Why?" she asked herself aloud. But she knew the answer. Her father had always limited her. He pushed her into impossible situations at the magazine, and drove her into the mold he wanted, but had never given her control at the ranch. "Magazines are for women," he said more than once. "Ranching is man's work!" And only now did Rachel Hammond see that that sort of statement was fuel for so many of her rages.

When Charlie came back about fifteen minutes later he was alone. "I only asked him a question," she said defensively. "I can't make heads nor tails out of these ledger books, so I only asked him a question. You'd think that the owner was entitled to a simple explanation, wouldn't you?'' She came up out of her chair and pushed it back so hard that it slammed into the wall and fell over.

''You would certainly think so.'' Charlie came straight to her, around the desk, past the chair's spinning little casters, holding his arms out. Without thinking, Rachel took that one step forward and was enveloped in the warmth.

They stood that way for about five minutes, until Rachel began to reason beyond the comfort and the warmth. She pushed herself away from him. He let her go without a struggle, bending down to set her chair back on its wheels. She sank into its safety with a sigh. ''Why did you do that?''

''Do what? Hug you?'' He tilted her chin upward, to where he could look into her eyes. ''You've never been hugged before?''

''Not much.''

''But you enjoyed it?''

''Yes.''

He sat down in the big chair in front of her desk. ''Hugging,'' he lectured, ''is a primal need for human beings. You said we ought to get to know each other better. There's no better way for that to happen than hugging.''

''Not kissing?''

''No, not kissing. Kissing builds up—other—tensions. Hugging is the thing, Ms. Rachel. Now then, about your Mr. Hendrix.''

''He—he's not really *my* Mr. Hendrix. He's my *father's* Mr. Hendrix. What about him?''

"He claimed that you didn't know beans about running a ranch. That your father never let you put a hand to ranching, not once."

"I—I'm afraid that's true. He wanted me to run the magazine, to make a lot of money that we could plow back into the ranch, and he—never——"

"That's all right," he interrupted. "It doesn't matter. Anyone can learn this business if she has a good teacher."

A tiny spark of independence returned to her. "And you're that teacher?"

"Well, that's up to you to say, Ms. Rachel. For the moment I can take over the work. You can evaluate it. If I don't make a difference in a month's time you can get someone else."

"I—don't like the way you said that." She sat up in her chair and sniffed a tear away. "You make it sound as if Mr. Hendrix is——"

"Leaving," he interrupted again. "After a sincere talk, Mr. Hendrix told me that he had worked long enough for the brand, and was going to quit."

"Oh, my! He—you just discussed it and he——"

"Threw in his hand, as Zane Gray would say. Effective yesterday."

"But—he's been working here a long time, and he ought to have a pension and retirement benefits, and things like that."

He grinned at her, and leaned across the desk to where the account books still lay. "Mr. Hendrix," he drawled, "has been collecting his retirement benefits for the past ten years or more."

"I don't understand."

"Those longhorns," he said, tapping the book with one finger. "I don't know when you bought them for fattening, or how long you've kept them, but they've been sold." His big finger tapped the cover of the book. "And I gather there hasn't been an entry made in the book. Mr. Hendrix and his two friends kept the sale money."

"But—that's——"

"You don't have any idea what you would get for twenty prime longhorns these days, do you? The long-horn is all lean beef. In this day of dieting, lean beef is the clamor from every supermarket in the country."

"You're right," she said. "I haven't any idea how much money is involved." So he told her.

"Dear God!"

"Exactly. Now, we could call the sheriff and have your Mr. Hendrix arrested for theft. Or we could give him a good kick in the seat of his pants and get him out of here. If we arrest him it will cause a good deal of scandal. If we boot him out, there'll be a lot less trouble."

Rachel Hammond was not a girl who required much time to make up her mind. "Do it."

"I did." Charlie rubbed the knuckles of his right hand. Rachel looked. The skin across that massive hand had been scraped.

"You didn't hurt him?"

"Not very much. He thought it was a great joke. Up until I carefully explained the whole situation. And then he got up and went over behind the barn to get his truck. As far as I know, he's halfway to Beaumont by this time."

"And those other two?"

"Would you believe, they turned out to be cousins of his? They left at the same time. After I finished the argument with Hendrix, the other two didn't seem to want to argue any further."

"I—you leave me with nothing more to say," she commented as she leaned back in her chair. It was a relief she had seldom felt, this leaning back to allow the chair to take up some responsibility. Her mother and father had taught her to sit with straight back and feet flat on the floor. I wonder if I...? she argued with herself. And then, "Oh, the devil with it."

She reached over and pulled out the top drawer of the desk. And then, with careful maneuver, put her heels up on the desk itself. The chair squeaked, she achieved balance, and suddenly the world was full of sunshine.

"I don't suppose you ever put your feet up on a desk?" she asked.

"Not when I'm wearing spurs," he returned. That broad grin was back on his face, rubbing out those grim lines that she associated with him. It made him look— somewhat—attractive. If there really were such a thing as love, Hammond, she lectured herself, this might be the sort of man to begin it with!

"Now then, Boss, what would you like me to do next?"

Her feet came off the desk with a dismal thump. "I thought we had straightened everything out," she said. "You're the foreman—and you'll figure out what's next. Won't you?"

The question at the end of the statement was said tentatively. She even managed to work up a tiny smile of encouragement, which seemed to set him off into a gale of laughter. Which she just could not understand.

When he finally quit the laughter he said, "Yes. I'll figure out what to do next, but you're the boss. You have to put your brand on all the goings-on. Like, we need a couple of hands right away."

"Okay. Hire some."

"I did. They'll be in tomorrow."

"Then," she said, "we need to conduct a muster, to see how many cattle we really have."

"Right on the spot," he returned. "Down in Texas we call it a roundup. For which we'll need a helicopter."

"Rent one?"

He put his feet up on the corner of the desk. Rachel emulated him. It felt so good. Not that she had her feet up, although that was a—relaxing—postion. But rather because she was, for the first time, feeling totally relaxed. Nothing seemed to be impossible.

"To tell the truth," he mused, "I already have a chopper in the area. I suppose we could use it until we get settled down?"

"It has to be business," she said. "No borrowings, no gifts. Straight business."

"Yup. Straight business."

"This is all very nice," she said in a brave tone of voice, "but it's not the major objective of your visit." He nodded as if he understood.

"When I said I wanted you to give me a baby I meant it." His eyes narrowed. "Of course, I meant it to be by artificial insemination!"

Charlie Mathers, caught unawares, almost choked as he lost his balance and his chair fell over onto the floor.

CHAPTER FOUR

THE ranch lay quiet for three days. Nothing stirred at the house. On occasion Rachel would come out to the stables, and Charlie would appear, unsummoned. Together they would saddle up, walk sedately out of the paddock, and then ride like the wind for as long and as far as her mare and his gelding would take them. On the afternoon of that third day Charlie borrowed her car and went off.

On the next day a helicopter circled the house a couple of times just an hour before lunch. The stabled horses snorted and jittered at the noise. Rachel came out of the office, a furrow on her face. A lesson in bookkeeping the night before had set her to searching this morning, and she did not like what she had read.

The noise of the chopper brought her outside, as the pilot searched for a flat place to land. The machine came down with a bump as a stray gust of wind struck the blades just at the moment of landing. The landing shocks squealed, the carriage absorbed the blow, and the giant blades lowered their pitch and finally came to a stop.

Even Mrs. Colchester was brought to the scene by her own curiosity. She stood on the veranda with a mixing bowl and wooden spoon in hand, and nagged at her mistress, whose immediate response was to run out into the yard, not at all a ladylike response.

"Charlie!"

He climbed awkwardly out of the cabin and came over to her. "You were expecting chopped liver?" He looked over his shoulder at the aircraft. "Seventeen years," he mused, "and I still can't get the landings right!"

"Don't be like that," Rachel said in her softest voice. "I don't doubt that you're the finest pilot in the—in the what? I missed you."

"One night and you missed me?" He chucked her under her chin and laughed. "Air Force, lady. Air Force." Henrietta came trotting out to meet them. He stooped to ruffle the dog's fur.

"The men ought to be along any minute," he said as he walked them back to the house.

"They came already," Mrs. Colchester reported. "Two men, two trucks, two trailers, two horses. And they are all Indians! Me, I am Indian too, of the Potowotami."

Charlie stretched out and laughed. It was the first time he had seen even the tiniest crack in the housekeeper's stolid face. "The horses are Indians too?"

"You know what I mean," the woman said, demanding with her eyes that her dignity be restored. "The men—they're not from any tribe around here."

"Comanche," he told her, and grinned as her black eyes grew rounder. "Comanche warriors. You'd better hide, little Potowotami."

"Don't tease her." Rachel Hammond had grown immeasurably over the past few days. She had a better control over both her reflexes and her emotions. But still there was that glint of rock-hard character in her eyes. Flint-hill character? she asked herself. Am I like the rock of these hills? It's nice to have him back. Very nice. But that doesn't mean I have to tell him so, or let him read it in my face.

"Lunch in ten minutes," she announced. Mrs. Colchester cut off her smile. Look at that, Rachel told

herself. She's been giving the orders for so long that she's
insulted when I usurp her place. Or maybe it's when I
regain the place that *she* usurped so long ago? In any
event, the housekeeper said nothing, but set off for the
kitchen, muttering, "Lunch in ten minutes. Hah!" under
her breath.

Charlie put his hands on Rachel's shoulders and turned
her into the light. "So. You look a lot better, boss. Been
out in the fresh air?"

"And curled up with a good book," she said solemnly. "The station accounts. We seem to have holes in
our fabric."

"About as big as the holes in your fences," he commented. And at that moment a heavy truck pulled up
into the yard, hesitated for a moment, and went off up
the hill. The sign on the side of the truck said Pontiac
Fence Menders.

"A separate crew for the fencing job," he reported as
she turned to look. "There's too much to do and cut a
tally too. You know the old story, the West was won by
colt revolvers and barbed wire fences? We don't need
the revolvers, but we do need the fences. Are you friendly
with all your neighbors?"

"Mostly. You'd better wash. There's been a revol-
ution in the kitchen, but being on time is still important."

He slid one of his big hands up behind her neck and
positioned her head for a quick kiss on the forehead.
He turned and walked down the hall toward the
bathroom, while Rachel's eyes followed him. That long,
loping stride, the cut of his square shoulders—everything a woman could ask for, she told herself, and then
grinned. Because of course he wasn't. He wasn't exactly
tall, he wasn't dark except for his permanent sunburn,
and she was positive that she could find somewhere on

his stripped torso some pure white. And he wasn't—well, that might be debated—handsome. He was very good at evading the issue in these parts. She brushed a hand across her forehead, where his lips had touched her. That was nice, wasn't it? Of course it was, you dope, she retorted, and went off to her own ablutions.

They were both back at the required time. Mrs. Clochester had set the table rather formally, including a pure white tablecloth. The dishes seemed to be a little more fancy than he had become accustomed to. "My grandmother's," Rachel explained.

"Makes me suspicious," he replied. "Usually when a restaurant improves the chinaware it's because the food is getting worse."

"Not worse," she said, teasing him. "But certainly different."

And so it was. When Mrs. Colchester wheeled in a cart of food, it contained a stack of hamburgers, a pot of steaming coffee, and a very small side dish of vegetables. "Wow," he said.

"Wow indeed. Mrs. C threatened to quit. Said it wasn't Christian to gorge yourself on red meat."

"You pacified her? A rise or something?"

"Hey," she said. "I read the books. I understand your system. Hendrix wasn't the only one working a good thing around here. I told her if she didn't straighten up and fly right I'd fire her. Now, what about the proposal I made to you a few nights ago?"

"I have to eat," he objected. "And then I have a mile of work to do. You'll just have to wait, Rachel."

She looked at him curiously. "Are you *sure* your brothers and sisters all have big families?"

"Every one," he said as he reached for a burger. "God's own truth. Every one."

"And you've never had any childhood—accidents?"

"Broke my leg once," he answered innocently.

"Damn you," she muttered. "A broken leg wouldn't affect this! I *have* to have an answer!"

"All in good time," he mumbled, his mouth full of burger. "My, isn't this stuff a lot better than watercress?"

The work was hard. First a helicopter sweep around the entire perimeter of the spread, with Rachel and one of the workmen from the wire crew in the back seat. "And there's another big one down there," Charlie said. The chopper heeled over to one side and dived like an attack machine. Rachel lost her arrogant cool and squealed, just before she lost all her color.

"Do you have to do that?" Said petulantly, as she bent over to hold her stomach together. He casually turned around in his seat to look.

"Don't do that," she commanded. "Look where you're—flying."

"I didn't realize you had stomach problems," he half apologized. "Did you get that location, Heinz?"

"Got it. That makes six. It hardly seems that there are any cattle at all on the spread. Most of them could walk their way to Topeka at the drop of the hat."

"Not to worry," Charlie said. "There's good grass and plenty of water in the central area. Cattle may not be the smartest animals in the world, but they seldom walk off and leave good grazing behind them. Under their own steam, that is. Now, one more stretch, and we'll have it."

"Then you wouldn't mind going just the least bit slower?"

He twisted around in his seat again and inspected her. Pale cheeks, perspiration, trembling hands. "No, I wouldn't mind. In fact, we'll go straight back to the house. That's plenty for today. It'll be two or three days before your crew can get all that.''

"Three," Heinz commented. "We follow the old Spanish tradition, '*poco a poco*.'''

"Which means?" Rachel managed to ask.

"A little bit at a time," Charlie told her, and then concentrated on the approach and a gentle landing. He did a better job of it this time, but Rachel needed help to unglue her fingers from the steel arms of her seat.

By dinnertime Rachel was exhausted. It was not an unusual thing, but normally it was mental exhaustion. This time it was physical. She groaned as Mrs. Colchester helped her into her chair.

"Some ancient and arcane Kansas disease?" Charlie came in, humming a little tune, and took the chair next to her. There are times, she told herself, when I deeply resent all that muscle of his. But then he wasn't down on hands and knees scrubbing the floor!

"Housecleaning," she retorted. "I hadn't realized how little cleaning has gone on in this house during the past few years. Mrs. Colchester assures me that she's the cook, not the housekeeper. I ache in places where I didn't even know I had places."

"I'll give you a good massage after we eat," he promised.

"No, thanks." She drew herself up straight-backed in her chair and glared at him. "Another one of your secret skills?"

"Yes." He gave a grand sigh. "My last one, I'm sorry to say. Good chicken, this is. Local stuff?"

"Yes." Her voice sparkled with pride. "Except for the fresh vegetables, we grow most everything we eat.

And what we don't grow—like flour, for instance—we trade for with our neighbors. This ranch ought to be self-sufficient.''

"Don't worry your head," he said. "Sooner 'n you can say 'jump' it will be!''

The next day she volunteered to go out on the range with him. "You won't like it," he promised. "Better if you stay at home. Most women don't exactly appreciate range work.''

"Well, I'm no candy heart," she said, and despite his objections she saddled her own horse and joined the crew just as the sun came up.

"The first thing we do," he told her, "is to gather a little herd together. The men built a corral out in the boondocks yesterday. Once we get the cattle into the enclosure, we'll go to work.''

"Seems to me the only work required is to move the cattle into the enclosure," she said. "What else can there be?''

"I . . ." He was almost ready to tell her, and decided not to. "I think you'd better wait and see," he said. So all morning long she rode trail as the men gathered in strays from the north section of the range. It wasn't as bad as she expected. From her reading, she expected a ride in a spit of dust. Here on the prairie, where the grass was as tall as a steer's stomach, there wasn't that much of a problem. By noon they had gathered in some fifty head.

She was glad when he swung down from his saddle and invited her to do the same. Mrs. Colchester had appeared, driving a wagon that was to serve as a chuck wagon. A fire improved the landscape. She hung on the rail of the temporary corral and looked at her bawling possessions.

"Not bad," he told her. "Take a good look. Those older steer look to be four years old. They're ready for market. Where do you ship them?"

"We generally move them by truck over to Holcombs," she told him. "The big slaughterhouse to the west of us."

"So we'll sell off those twenty-two," he said, whittling another notch on the tally stick which seemed to be always with him. "Do you have any idea what they'll bring?"

"Not the slightest," she said. "I can quote you advertising rates for any page and size in our magazine, but ranch prices... Mr. Hendrix always took care of that."

"What an owner," he chided. "Those are all prime beef." And he told her what price she might expect. Rachel took a deep breath. It was almost as if Santa Claus had scheduled a second visit to the hill country all in one year.

"And now what about those others?" She gestured at the rest of the herd that was gradually being segregated.

"I don't understand this," he allowed. "Normally when you buy young beef and fatten it, you don't have this sort of problem. But there are young calves out there. They need to be branded. And then..." His voice dropped, as if he didn't want her to hear.

"What?"

"Rachel," he said, "come get your lunch."

"I'd like to know what's going on. It's my ranch."

"It certainly is," he agreed. "But after lunch, shall we?"

Back at the chuck wagon, Mrs. Colchester had arranged a canvas fly-leaf which provided a little shade at the side of the wagon. They all moved into that shade, collected a plateful of food, and squatted down to eat.

"Don't you think this meal is a little too hearty?"

He looked over at her plate. "We're not writing gossip stories," he told her. "Beef stew, with plenty of vegetables. Just right for this kind of work. Plenty of hot grub. Eat up." Just this once, Rachel told herself, I'm not going to argue with him. He's been nice to me for a couple of days so I'll be nice to him.

She stuffed herself, and then added a little more. When the meal was done he walked over to the spring near where they were camped, filled both canteens, and came back. By that time the two cowboys were inside the corral, with a separate fire going.

"I want to see," she insisted.

He pulled her down to the ground. "No, you don't," he said. She could smell the sizzle of hide as the branding irons were put to use. The heifers bawled and kicked up a fuss. Sitting behind the chuck wagon as they were, she could see nothing.

"I thought that branding wasn't supposed to hurt them?" she asked anxiously.

"Depends on how thick the hide is," he returned.

"Have you any idea how cruel that sounds?" she asked, exasperated. "How would you feel if somebody came around and tried to put their brand on your—your hindquarters? That's no way to treat a lovely little cow."

"You just aren't going to let go, are you?" he said wryly. "Well, in order of questions, no, I wouldn't care to have my bum branded. Secondly, the heifers aren't the ones making all the noise."

"That's enough evasion," she snapped. For a moment she was Hammond, back again in all her regal glory. "Tell me what's going on!"

"Okay, lady, you asked for it. Some of those little beasts are male."

"That doesn't tell me anything!"

"You're in the business of fattening cattle," he said, sighing. "The male is a fractious animal. If you want him to be fat and contented you have to——"

"Oh, my God, they aren't——"

"Yes, they are, ma'am. Would you like to go watch?"

Rachel certainly didn't want to go and watch. She didn't even want to stay where she was. She was up on her feet before he could offer a hand, dashing away from the wagon and the corral, in the direction of the spring. By the time he caught up with her she had lost all her lunch, and was hunched over in some misery, trying to comfort her upset stomach.

To complete her misery, she was still crouched down next to the spring when the two cowboys came out of the corral. "All finished, Charlie," one of them said. "We're going to have a fine meal of prairie oysters tonight. Care to come join us?"

"Prairie oysters?" she asked.

"They're going to stay out here tonight," he said. "The trucks will be available tomorrow morning. After they load them up they'll round up another bunch, and do it all over again."

"Prairie oysters?" she demanded. He had been trying to avoid looking at her. Now it was impossible. Her face was white, her eyes rimmed with red, and she was trembling.

"Take my word for it," he said. "Nothing is wasted at a roundup. You really wouldn't want to know."

"Oh, my God." She came up to her feet, looking for some place to run. Nothing appeared appetizing, so she moved a tentative foot in his direction, and then ran at him as soon as he opened his arms to her.

Mrs. Colchester had finished hitching her old piebald horse to the chuck wagon, and started to bump over the prairie toward the ranch house. "Come on," he ordered.

Without protest, Rachel Hammond went with him to where their horses had been ground looped, and waited while he saddled them both. They rode back, a full hour of travel, without a word being said. When she dismounted at the stable she left him to care for the horses, and fled to the house.

At dinnertime Charlie was the only one to come to the table. Mrs. Colchester grumbled and mumbled as she served him. A fine, full meal it was, but the cook was certainly not happy. About an hour later she came to him, on her way home.

"Ms. Hammond, she would like to see you right away in her office," she said. "It was fun to be out on the range today. Missy didn't like it?"

"How right you are." He pulled himself to his feet and finished off the bottle of beer at his elbow. "Missy sure didn't like it."

Despite the "right away" he took his time, poured himself a second cup of coffee from the carafe on the side table, and only when that was finished did he stretch, and start down the corridor.

The office door was closed. He knocked peremptorily and went in without waiting for an invitation. The woman behind the desk looked up at him. Not exactly the Hammond of *Gossiper* fame, and yet not exactly Rachel, who was filled with fears and complexes.

"You wanted to see me?"

"Yes, I can't wait much longer, Charlie." She nervously brushed her hair off her forehead, and planted both feet firmly on the floor. This time, she told herself, we're going to settle everything. Everything important, that is. He's not going to weasel out of it. It's not too late for me to go back to Libertyville and get the second man on the list.

Oh, isn't it? Of course it's too late. There's more to him than just being the father of my child. He's a multiple character, and somehow I seem to like all of him! Fool!

He dropped into the chair in front of her, draping one long leg over the chair arm. "Now just what was that you can't wait for?"

"Don't give me that business," she snapped. Strange how easily he brought the onslaught of tears to her eyes. But not this time, she told herself. Not this time. "You know darn well I'm talking about—my baby! Now, are you in agreement?"

He hesitated, looking her up and down. "Don't you think this is kind of crazy?" he asked. "With your magazine and this spread, how are you going to take care of a baby? I'll bet you don't even know where to begin."

"I can learn," she muttered through clenched teeth. "Other women have managed, without a lot of education. I can learn. There are books. I can take courses at the university. What is there that's so difficult?"

"It's more than just changing diapers or filling bottles," he said bleakly. "You also have to love them. Not your strong suit, is it?"

She whirled around in her swivel chair so that her back was to him. But not fast enough so that he could not see the tear forming in her eyes.

Low blow, he told himself. Hammond may be impenetrable, but Rachel is as vulnerable as the day is long. She's not crying about a baby; she's crying about a life without love! For just a moment Charlie Mathers realized something that had been hiding away inside him. For all his years in the service, for all his large family, he was a little short in the loving field himself. He was about to add on to the conversation, when she wheeled her chair around, her eyes blazing.

"Damn you!" she exploded. "I suppose you think you have a monopoly on loving?" He held up two hands in surrender, but she kept right at him. "If I had a child, I could take care of him. Who would know better than me how hard it is for a child to grow up without love?" A pause for a surreptitious wipe at her leaking eye. "And I'm *going* to have a baby!"

"Look," he replied, "I don't have any objection to your having a baby. As the last of the Hammonds, I suppose you owe it to your father and his father to do something. But tell me again why I should be the father of this child?"

"Because," she sputtered, "because you've been carefully selected by my doctor to be the perfect match. Genetically, physically, mentally, everything. And, I've already told you, I'll pay you well for the service."

"Ah. You've been running a stud book on me?"

"You're darn well right," she said grimly. "This child is too important to me to be left to chance. And don't bother me with all those arguments about how millions of women managed to get it done without all this trouble. I'm not millions of people. There's only one of me— the last Hammond. I have to be careful." A moment's pause, and then she added plaintively, "And even with all this search and testing—I don't understand. You don't seem to be—you almost react as if you weren't the man we tested."

"Sort of a mockingbird egg left in the nest?" For just a second Charlie considered telling the truth about how he had come into the system by accident, short-circuiting the Hammond Search and Seizure program. But only for a second. His uncle, before he died, had wanted mightily for him to come north and help this girl-woman. And Uncle Roger had been important in Charlie's growing up. He nodded.

"All right. I guess I could—theoretically—agree to the proposal."

"Good! I'll get the medical team out here tomorrow, and they can get it over with in a jiffy."

"Now whoa," he objected. "Just slow down. I said I can see this being a reasonable idea—in theory. But when you come right down to earth, I don't know that I can agree, not at all. Artificial insemination?"

"I can't believe you're saying that," she told him. "It's by far the most scientific way of doing it. The ranches use the technique all the time. That's why one bull can service a complete herd of cows. I can't see your objection." She settled back in her chair. *So there!* she told herself. There isn't a better way to get this done. Not one!

"So tell me why," he pondered, "you would want to have one bull service a complete herd. Are there more of you hidden in some corner?"

"I—no." Damn you! She was almost out of her chair before common sense took over. So he's playing hard to get?

"No, there's only me. That was only a metaphor. I'll up the price fifty percent."

"Sounds better and better all the time," he answered.

He's weakening, she told herself. I've got him pinned down! "But?" she asked. "There was a *but*?"

"Indeed there was," he said, rising. "You've got the wrong bull—er—man, Ms. Hammond. That's the trouble with all this research. Sure, artificial insemination is great for the rancher. Probably the cows don't mind in the least. But did anyone ever ask the bull what *he* felt about the situation?"

"You don't make a great deal of sense," she commented. "It's all very simple. I don't see why we have to introduce all this emotionalism into a simple business proposition. Surely you don't expect us to go back to the old-fashioned——"

"But that's exactly what I *do* mean," he interrupted. "If you want me to cooperate, ma'am, it's back to the old-fashioned groaning and moaning and sweat proposition. And there's no other way that I'm willing to cooperate."

She was up out of her chair, her mouth formed for the usual Hammond roar, but no sound came out. What's wrong with me? she asked herself. I don't dare roar at him. He might walk out on me. So? So, said a deeper intelligence within her, I don't want to go through with this with some other man. Just with him. Which isn't logical! You might think I'm doing something emotional and stupid—like falling in love?

"Charlie, sit down. Surely we two logical human beings can reason our way through to a better solution?"

"None that I can think of," he said. "Look, ma'am. I'm tired. It's been a long, tough day, and I need some rest. That's my best offer. If you want me to father your child, then we do it the old-fashioned way."

"But—that could take months." She sighed. "Although I've never tried it, I understand it to be very—

vulgar. And there's no certainty of—being successful.
There's no accounting for how often—I—surely you
don't mean that, Charlie?''

"I surely do," he returned. "You have some very fine
arguments, Rachel, about the cow and the crowd and
the convenience. But I have to look at it strictly from
the viewpoint of the bull. If you have some scientific
survey that tells me the bull enjoys the hell out of all
this, I'll rethink things. But until then, lady, it has to be
the old-fashioned way. And now, if you'll pardon me,
I'll get to bed."

She watched his back as he stalked out of the room.
An angry back, as if she had insulted him, she thought.
And all I've tried to do is to get some common sense
into this proposition. Surely there's no need to go
through all that tangle of emotions that he seems to
want? No doubt about it; I ought to go back to town
and get my advisers to send me the number two man on
the list. But—could they find a man who could take care
of me *and* my ranch's problems? Could they find a man
so full of humor and care and concern? Not just for me,
but for everything and everybody? And if they could,
would *I* be able to think about this new person the way
I think about *dear Charlie?*

Wasn't that a dead giveaway? *"Dear* Charlie." I can't
believe it. After all the years of lecture from my father,
have I fallen off the bandwagon of stoic logic in just a
couple of weeks? *"Dear* Charlie"? Come on now,
woman, think straight. How does he rate such a salu-
tation? Of course, I call Henrietta *"dear"* as well. A
short form for affection, I suppose. And I *never* think
to call Mrs. Colchester *"dear."* Doesn't that tell you
something, Rachel Hammond? I wonder what he would
say if he knew I'm classifying him in the same group as

my dog? Now if I can only hold to that picture I ought
to be able to break out of this problem about the bull!
And now let's go to bed. "Perchance to dream"?

Charlie started out for his bedroom, but detoured into
the shower. One shower was not enough in the ranching
business. He had a terrible itch in the middle of his
back—and another one somewhere else. Neither could
be scratched! "Damn woman," he muttered as he
climbed into the hot spray and turned to get the right
angle of attack. "Why me, God?"

The hot water soothed. He applied a liberal dose of
soap, massaging it in almost subconsciously, and
thinking. Rachel Hammond. "There's no doubt," he
muttered to himself, "that she's one hell of a lot of
woman. Point number one." Another liberal soaping.
"There's no doubt that she wants—what? Not me,
perhaps, but the service I can offer. And isn't that a
terrible way to think about this woman? As if she were
a cow, waiting to be serviced. But isn't that exactly what
she keeps saying? Well, they're not going to fool around
with *my* family jewels with all this artificial insemination business!"

Despite all his complaints, at this moment he found
things were running out of control. He flipped off the
hot water and let the cold run down his big frame. By
the time he dried off he was still incensed, but somewhat
calmer.

Why did this broad pick me up and proposition me?
And who is this doctor that she keeps referring to?
Somebody I *should* have met? The idea teased at him
as he walked down the hall. Some fancy plan of
Hammond's which came unhitched? Is there, some-
where in the wide, wide world, a big hulk of a man,

CHAPTER FIVE

RACHEL failed to make an appearance at the breakfast table. Mrs. Colchester, coming in with the syrup for the pancakes, shook her head. "Very bad," she said. "The nose runs, the eyes weep, the throat coughs. I don't understand it. She spends all night on the porch, you understand. Something about worshiping the stars. I don't know this worship. She says, after you have breakfasted, would you please to come by her bedroom for just a moment?"

"Yes, of course," Charlie replied as he dug into the succulent pancakes. "If she's not coming, I suppose I could eat all of this by myself?"

"It would make me very happy," Mrs. Colchester said with a little giggle. "Always she worries about the food. Waste not, want not, she says. And things like that."

"Well, I'm glad somebody's happy around this place. Run along now, child."

"Not a child," the woman replied firmly. "At sixty I am not a child!"

"Yes. Yes, of course you're not. Sixty, huh? How long have you been on the ranch?"

"I came when I was young. With the grandfather, you understand. Maybe I was—oh—thirteen then."

"And you never had the chance to finish school?"

The woman turned around to face him. "Always this question," she said. "Why should I finish school? Do they teach you how to live, how to ranch, how to find a husband? Nothing. My father said I must learn more.

looking for this woman? The idea tickled him so much that he was laughing as he passed Rachel's closed door.

Rachel, who was still awake, despite her every attempt not to be so, heard him come down the hall. His footsteps hesitated for a moment outside her door, and then he laughed and went on down toward his own room.

Damn the man, she thought. Double damn him! She had pulled and pushed and tossed for so long already that her sheets were tangled around her and she had lost her pillow somewhere. Indignantly she squeezed herself off onto the floor, threw her blankets back on the bed and stomped over to her window. It was one of those clear, cool Kansas nights. The stars in their myriads were sparkling overhead. A three-quarter moon changed the whole outside world to silver. That wary coyote up on the ridge was joined by a partner, both wailing to the skies. A mating call? Rachel felt a shiver run up her spine. The last time she had thought of mating calls was when she was fourteen, watching an old Rin-Tin-Tin movie on television.

Disgusted, she fumbled around in the dark for her robe, and managed to wrap it around her. There might be peace out in the open. Certainly there was none to be found in her bedroom. She opened her door carefully, to avoid waking him, and walked down the hall to the kitchen door.

A cool, almost cold wind was blowing when she stepped out of the house. She closed the door as quietly as she could, then walked around the corner of the veranda to where the lounge chairs waited. Rachel Hammond, restless in body and soul, tried to discipline herself, without any luck. She paced back and forth for a time, then returned to the chairs and dropped into one of them.

There were incidental noises from the barn. The chink of some sort of metal, the casual stomping of a stabled horse, and the sound of water, flowing from the little spring that provided water for both house and barn. Somewhere in the distance she heard a mournful birdcall. A loon? The wind ruffled her hair. She relaxed for a moment.

Her left hand was hanging down, almost touching the floor. A cold, wet nose thrust itself into it. "Blue?"

Not the puppy, but the mother. "Henrietta?" Her fingers were licked in acknowledgment. "Only us women keeping the night watch?" Her dog gruffed an agreement. "Well, we deserve each other, don't we?" Another agreement.

"Am I being a fool, dog? I know all there is to know about running a gossip rag. Why the devil am I dreaming of remaking myself into a rancher? Instead of using that psychologist to find me a man, I should have used some man to find me a psychologist!"

Her dog snorted in disgust and lay down to sleep. "And that," Rachel told herself, "is just what I need too. Tomorrow I will put on the whole armor of innocence—Lord, where did *that* phrase come from?—and completely neglect this Texas cowpoke. I'll get another good week of rest, and then go back to the magazine. Maybe I'll leave him out here to run the ranch. He seems to be pretty good at what he does. Horses, cattle, choppers—now don't say that didn't surprise you, Rachel Hammond!"

She squirmed around, trying to make herself comfortable in the lounge chair, but the wind was rising,

the temperature dropping, and neither her nig[ ] her robe did much to alleviate her feelings.

So stop playing the heroine, she told herself[ ] back into the house for something warm. She[ ] herself out of the chair, waking the dog in the [ ] and stopped for a moment to apologize. By the [ ] Henrietta was finished with her objections, Rachel [ ] really chilled. She fumbled for her slippers, but co[ ] only find one. It was a hop and a skip routine acro[ ] the wood floor of the veranda, until finally she came t[ ] the door. Henrietta was close behind her.

Rachel fumbled for the knob. The door was old, the knob was older, and it normally required a considerable slam to open it. So, without thinking, Rachel gave the knob a hard twist, and pushed against the door with her shoulder. And nothing happened.

"Oh, Lord," she muttered. She knew without looking. The Yale snap lock had closed when she came out of the house, and there was no way in the world that sh[ ] could get back in. Except to go around the house a[ ] tap on Charlie's window. And that, she told hersel[ ] will never do. So back she went to the lounger, inv[ ] Henrietta to come up with her to share the heat[ ] prepared to spend the rest of the night consortin[ ] the stars.

"But you see," she told herself, "if I were [ ] terms with Charlie, all of this would be a lau[ ] was a good moral lesson, but did nothing towa[ ] her warm through the night.

Poor Indians are always poor if they have not the education. But Mr. Hammond, he says a woman only needs
to know house and home and kitchen. So, he offers more
money, and I stay. I send it all back home, and my father,
he don't argue any more. *You* finish school?''

Caught unprepared, Charlie blinked at the attack.
"Well, I guess I'd have to say yes," he confessed. "I
finally finished college. It took me six years to do it, but
it's done. Can't you see that I *look* smarter now?''

The woman giggled again. Charlie shook his head,
disgusted at his own action. A giggle, from an Indian
woman, did not mean what it meant to a white woman.
It meant she was embarrassed by the subject.

"Foolish talk," she returned. "Going to school does
not show on the outside, only on the inside. You don't
forget, Ms. Rachel says come to see her?''

"I won't forget. A very educational conversation, Mrs.
Colchester." The woman giggled again and fled. Charlie
turned back to his plate to give the pancakes the greeting
they deserved.

Rachel Hammond sat up in her narrow bed, two pillows
plumped up behind her. Her nose was red and sore, her
eyes were blurred, and she had a massive headache. All
emphasized by her sense of having been ill-used.
Nevertheless she was dressed, if one might call it that,
in one of those frilly nightgowns that her Aunt Harriet
had bought for her, back in the days when her brother
Jimmy was still the heir apparent, and little Rachel was
just a happy-go-lucky girl. The clothes were still stuffed
in the back of her cupboard, and she hadn't heard from
Aunt Harriet in almost ten years. But today, for some
reason, she had ordered Mrs. Colchester to dig this rag
out for her. A pure white cotton gown, almost trans-

parent, that covered everything from chin to ankles, and yet left everything exposed. She could barely see herself in the mirror on the opposite wall, but she tried to preen. That was the moment he came through the half-opened door with his usual casual approach. Unless one studied his eyes, one would think he had not noticed the gown at all. Damn the man, Rachel told herself.

"I hear you're not feeling too well?"

He took the chair beside her bed, without even an invitation. I don't know why I bother, Rachel thought. He's not the least bit conformable. If I take up with this man, he'll have to be house-trained!

"I'm well enough to conduct business," she muttered, and then coughed a time or two to prove it. "Hammonds don't all go soft just because they have a little head cold!" Two more coughs, and a vain attempt to blow her nose without applying that hurtful pressure to it, without success.

"I have a feeling," he drawled, "that now I'm going to find out that it's all my fault."

"It is," she snapped. "Among the dozen or more things you repaired in the past few days was the lock on the kitchen door!"

"It needed it," he agreed, trying to maintain a neutral position. He knew by the set of her eyes that he was sailing, like the ancient Greeks, between Scylla and Charybdis on a wild sea.

She threw him a quick glance. "And locked me out in the cold. But that isn't what I asked you to stop by for."

"Oh?" He crossed his legs.

"I wanted to tell you," she said hurriedly, "that I've decided to agree to your terms."

"You agree to——?"

"You either have the worst memory or the lowest sex libido of any man I've ever met," she snapped.

"Oh, that." A moment's pause as if he was thinking something over. She glared at him, trying to compel him by the sheer power of her thoughts. Don't, she told herself, almost screaming. Don't introduce half a dozen other qualifications. Just say——

"Yes," he said, interrupting her thoughts. "Okay, then."

"That's it? Just 'okay'? Something as important as this, and all you have to say is 'okay'?" It was hard to control rage, Rachel discovered in that moment, when you were feeling as bad she was at that moment. I think every muscle in my body aches, and even some of the aches have aches! And this imperious—cowpoke—all he can do is slouch there and say "okay" on the most important decision in my life!

"Well," he said cautiously, "that seemed to be the important thing to say."

"And when," she asked, in a very unsteady voice, "can we arrange to get this—show on the road?"

"Most any day now," he allowed as he stood up. "It's not the sort of thing you can do when one partner is sickly, you know."

"When, damn you?"

"There's lots of things need doing around this spread," he told her. "Some more trouble with the cattle, for example. I plan to ride out to the tally and see what the problem is."

"And then there are, I suppose, half a thousand other things more important?"

"Matter of priorities, ma'am."

"Don't call me ma'am!"

"Yes, ma'am." He was out of the door before her dirty coffee cup smashed against the wall about six inches from his head. He whistled as he went down the hall, which only added to Rachel's tremendous headache.

The headache persisted throughout the day, made worse when Charlie bustled in at lunchtime, still whistling, and failed to come by the sickroom to report. Rachel fumed and fussed and tossed and turned. She wanted to ask him what was going on. She wanted to ask *somebody* about the editorial for this week's *National Gossiper*. She wanted to ask someone why her head hurt so much. She wanted to be somebody's little girl, allowed to climb up into somebody's comfortable lap and seek solace. She wanted to—murder that man?

Mrs. Colchester came in twice. Once to take her temperature, all the while muttering that she was hired to cook, not to run a nursing home. The second time with a large glass of hot lemonade, "Which is what my mother used all the time for colds, before Kansas was full of doctors. Quacks, the lot of them. Now see if you can drink the whole thing down."

Rachel managed the dose, and much to everybody's surprise fell into a uneasy sleep. When she awoke it was dark outside, and she was feeling as miserable as a girl could possibly be. So much so that she was unable to stop the shivering and the sobbing.

Charlie had spent the evening in the business office, where the paperwork was helping him develop a headache of his own. He walked quietly down the hall on his way to bed, when he heard Rachel crying. It was just the sort of thing he would never have expected from Hammond. He stopped by her door for a moment, and then went in.

By the feeble light of the night lamp he could see that Rachel was tossing and turning, her nightgown rumpled up to her thighs, her blankets all over the floor. She was mumbling. He tiptoed over to the bed and touched her forehead. It was warm and dry. Too warm. As well he knew, the nearest doctor was thirty-five miles away. Decisions, he told himself. Take her to the doctor? Bring the doctor to her? Compromise?

It was long after Mrs. Colchester had left the farmhouse, so what must be done lay entirely in his hands. First, she had to be made more comfortable. He searched the kitchen and came up with an enameled washbasin, which he filled with warm water and then carried back to the sickroom. "Rachel?"

She moaned something that he was unable to interpret. He shrugged his shoulders and went to work. Stripping her was no easy thing. The nightgown fitted just a little too closely everywhere. Once, during the exercise, she mumbled, "What are you doing?" He recited some doggerel that satisfied her, and when the nightgown was disposed of he gently laved her from head to toe. It was remarkable what effect the gentle washing had on the patient. And on him.

Rachel gradually settled down and accepted his ministrations. He himself required a considerable amount of discipline. She was a great deal of woman, and he was a man with a hair-trigger in the sex line. But, with all the handicaps, he finally managed to finish the job, change the sheets, and tuck her into a simple man's shirt to serve for the rest of the night.

During all of this she had managed to grab at his hand and hold it. Now, when he tried to break away, she stirred uneasily and refused to let go. "Don't leave me," she muttered. And then, more loudly, with a sense of panic, "Don't leave me!"

"I won't," he told her. That was before he assessed her narrow little bed. "I don't intend to sit up all night," he murmured.

"Don't leave me," she said, more clearly this time.

All of which seemed to leave only one alternative. He slipped his arms under her dead body weight and picked her up. "That's nice, Daddy," she whispered in his ear. Like a face full of water, that statement. Very suddenly he lost all his wild male responses, and managed to carry her back to his own room almost as if she were a child, kicking the door shut behind them.

Charlie had never disputed his room asssignment. It was probably the biggest bedroom in the house, with an immense, old-fashioned brass bed big enough for three. He overcame the difficulty of opening up the bed by balancing her weight on his knee while he pulled the blankets back. Throughout all this he kept crooning to her—fragments of songs that he had used for years when night-riding a herd of cattle. When finally he managed to get her down on one side of the bed, he chuckled to see that she was quiet, and wearing a big smile on her face.

He touched her forehead one more time. After an initial period of perspiration while he was bathing her, her temperature seemed to have dropped. And now what? he asked himself. It had been a long, hard day out on the range. Never had he known a more cantankerous herd. And one of the newly repaired sections of fence had come down and had to be repaired.

Accident? Poor installation? His wire repair team had come well recommended, but *seeing* was better than *thinking*, as his father used to say. Get to bed. Either

the problems of the night would go away, or they
wouldn't. There was no reason to stand in the middle
of the bedroom in the developing chill.

Back to the bathroom, feeling his way along the wall
to avoid putting on more lights. It gave him a chuckle.
He and Rachel were the only two living things left in the
house, give or take a mouse or two. A quick, warm
shower relaxed his muscles. His mind wandered. This
wasn't what he had planned when he came out of the
service. There was a small ranch over by Nogales way
that hadn't paid in over a decade. He had planned to
change that situation.

But now Rachel had his promise. Fathering her child
was not a one-night stand. Or even a nine-month stand.
If she bore his child, he meant to stick around to help
raise the little fellow. Yes, it would be a boy—Hammond
would, some way or another, see to that. And she would
expect, once the child was born, to give him a certificate
or something, and see him to the door. "And *I'll* see to
that," he grumbled as he shut off the water.

A heavy rub with the big bath towel, and, wearing
only the towel around his waist, he walked back down
the corridor to his own bedroom. There was a little bit
of light from the east windows, luckily, or he would have
fallen over his own boots. Another moment of contem-
plation, looking down into the darkness where she lay.
Well, he told himself wryly, she's been inviting me into
her bed for a long time!

He climbed into the bed, trying to be quiet, and not
succeeding. His two hundred and nine pounds were
somewhat more than the old springs were prepared for.
They complained. He froze in position, half up and half
down. Rachel stirred and muttered something. He hardly
caught a word. Something to do with the magazine—a

dream from the heart, he told himself. And then he relaxed the rest of the way. He flipped the towel off on to
the chair next to the bed, made himself a little nest as
far away from the sleeping girl as he could, and closed
his eyes.

Just after midnight, as restless as the cattle which had
made up most of his life, he came awake. The girl had
moved closer to him, turned on her side facing him, and
her head was resting on his shoulder.

Not quite comfortable, she wiggled a little further in
his direction. He managed to put his arm around her
shoulder for comfort's sake. The firm cones of her
breasts, separated from his skin by only a sheer cotton
shirt, bore into his chest. Charlie Mathers barely contained himself. Trapped in position where he lay, he could
neither come nor go. All he *could* do was lie still and
hope she wouldn't awaken and demand an explanation.

She made some delightful noise, and then giggled. Try
counting sheep, he advised himself, but being a true
cowhand he ended up counting steers. One after the
other, counting the north ends of Texas longhorns going
south through a hole in the barbed wire fence. Maybe
there's some symbolism there, he told himself. Even he
could hardly stand it. The tension wore him down, and
eventually he went to sleep.

Rachel Hammond woke up at about eight o'clock. Late
for her, but things were in such a jumble. To begin with,
there was a man in her bed, and her head was resting
on his shoulder. It took a lot of Hammond courage not
to scream. There *has* to be some logical explanation, she
told herself, as one of her fingers gently caressed his chin.

Man. Of course it was a man. He needed a shave. His
hair was tousled, giving him a boyish look. There was

a tiny scar just on the height of his right cheekbone. There was another below his right ear. Rachel shook her head. Not boyish—piratical! Be more careful in your judgments, woman!

Edge away from him. Get out before the volcano erupts! Obediently she edged. He made a muffled groan of protest, and the arm under her shoulder tightened, and then relaxed. But his other arm came over, landing one huge hand on her capacious left breast. Landed, cupped, coddled, and weighed. Another sigh—of enjoyment? Disgusted with herself, Rachel tore herself away with one quick roll, landing on the floor for her efforts. Or rather on his boots, set upright on the floor next to the bed, with his spurs next to the boots. Not the sharp-pointed rowels which could penetrate a horse's thick skin, but the round, blunt kind. Rachel's soft bottom had not the staying power for this or any other type of spur. She landed on them—sat on them, to be truthful, and this time it hurt. She screamed.

The bedroom door slammed open. Mrs. Colchester and her broom stood there. "What's going on here?" the woman yelled as she crossed the threshold with her broom raised to the attack position. The noise was too much for Charlie. He came awake, thoughts reverting to the war he had been fighting not more than six months before, and came up out of the bed, totally naked, ready to fight.

Mrs. Colchester screamed again. Rachel, not willing to be left out, struggled to her feet, gently comforting her punctured bottom.

"Charlie!" Rachel yelled, and motioned toward the bed. He took one look at his display of maleness and vaulted back under the covers again.

"I am not," Mrs. Colchester stated firmly, "going to continue working in this den of iniquity. Not one moment. How could you do this, Rachel Hammond? What would your father say? What would your grandfather say? Shame! Shame!"

"I haven't any idea what father would say," Rachel said gently. "As for Grampa, I suspect he would have said something like 'It's about time, girl!' He wasn't the saint you try to make him, Mrs. Colchester." Despite her ire, the cook pushed a chair over to her. Rachel fell into it, strangely relieved. I'm tired, she told herself. As weak as a kitten. What in the world has happened to me? Her eyes strayed to where Charlie was sitting up in the bed, his bottom half covered by the sheets, his top half, muscles and all, nude. Rachel drew a quick breath. Is that what happened to me? she asked herself. They say it's a very physical activity. He's worn me out, and I didn't even know it! Damn that man.

"That's enough, Mrs. Colchester," she ordered. "There's nothing of which Charlie or I should be ashamed. If you don't feel you can continue here, then pack your bags. I'll figure your wages right away."

"Well, of all the nerve," the cook sputtered. "Turning me off without a minute's notice after I've served your father and your grandfather—all those years?"

"I didn't turn you off, you quit," Rachel told her. "I'm sorry that your strict sensibilities have been bruised, but I can't help that. I can't even promise that it won't happen again. Now, are you going or staying?"

"That does it. I'm leaving. Immediately. At once!"

"Your paycheck will be on the desk in the office," Rachel told her. The woman glared at them both as she started out of the door. "You'll be sorry," she said. "The Lord punishes sinners!"

"If it is a sin, it's a very tiny one," Charlie responded.

"You are all," Mrs. Colchester said in a prophetic voice, "going straight to hell and damnation!" She slammed the door behind her. Rachel could hear her feet pounding down the hall.

"Well?" Charlie asked.

"Perhaps." Rachel sighed. "You make a great deal of trouble for just one man. I'd better get down to the office and figure out her pay."

"First things first," Charlie said. "She can wait. My stomach can't. Why don't you zoom down to the kitchen and whip us up some breakfast?"

"I would," Rachel Hammond said as she used one hand to push her hair back in place. "The only trouble is that I've never learned how to cook!"

The two of them gathered in the kitchen an hour later, prepared to do battle. "Me, I can cook steak," Rachel offered. "Mrs. Colchester likes to have help, but only for fetching and carrying. She guards her cooking secrets, you understand. But I spied long enough to cook a steak."

"Well, I can do steak and eggs," Charlie chimed in. "Standard range food. Lord knows there's always plenty of beef available on a cattle ranch. I hear chickens every morning somewhere around here."

"Which Mrs. Colchester always looked after," Rachel added glumly. "Out behind the barn there's a big chicken coop. I have no idea how many birds there are. Mrs. Colchester feeds them grain once a day. She gathers the eggs in the morning. Sometimes there aren't any eggs. When a hen goes for too many days without eggs, then we have a chicken dinner. The grain is in a big sack out in the barn."

"So I guess, Rachel, that you'll have to take over all that part of things until Mrs. Colchester gets over her peeves. Does she do this often?"

"Counting this time?" she asked. He nodded. "Well, in that case, she's blown up like this once in my lifetime."

He shook his head, with just a touch of a grin on one corner of his mouth. She glared at him. She had donned one of her prettiest outfits in honor of the occasion. A red and white dirndl blouse, low and square cut, offering a fine view of the tops of her breasts, matched with a calico skirt that swirled when she moved. He had already noticed the view. She had caught him at it the moment he came into the kitchen.

"Let me explain," she said, hiding her temper with a great deal of difficulty. "I was raised to be the editor of a magazine. I do that work very well. I live in a penthouse apartment at the Sheridan hotel. The hotel has a kitchen. When I order things they appear, already cooked. My dad said you only have so much room in your brain, so don't try learning things you don't need to know. I didn't need to know cooking. I still don't!"

"Well said." Charlie chuckled, which caused Rachel to lose just another bit of her temper. "So we'll have steak and eggs today. You scoot out and find us some eggs. I'll get the beef—we *do* have a side of beef aging?"

Rachel shrugged her shoulders. "In the cold room in the back of the house," she suggested. "I think we'd better hire somebody, or go back to the hotel."

Those eyes of his followed her, pinned her against the serving counter as if she were a butterfly in his collection. "We don't quit at the drop of a hat," he said. There was a hardness in his voice that she hadn't heard before, and she flinched away from it. "You talk about self-reliance, raising a baby all by yourself, but you can't see your way clear to spend a couple of weeks without kitchen help? Come on, girl."

"I can't eat steak and eggs for breakfast," Rachel complained. "The eggs are all right for occasional meals. The steak is too heavy. I need roughage. Cereals, milk, things like that."

"That stuff is easy to prepare," Charlie said. "Cereal comes in box. You put it in a bowl, and add milk."

"I don't think we have more than a pint of milk," she told him.

"And we don't have any cows in season?"

"Pasteurized milk," Rachel insisted. "After all, we have to be careful. I'm eating for two now."

He came around the table and stopped about a foot in front of her. What did I say? she asked herself. Did I sprout horns or something?

"Milk. Pasteurized milk," she repeated.

"The milk part I understand," he drawled. "Oh, hell. So somebody has to go into the town for food? How far?"

"Thirty miles. Down to Beaumont. Once a week. Mrs. Colchester used to go. I can find an old shopping list." Rachel backed away from him. That stern look was still in control of his face. The little scar seemed to be pulsing at her like a beacon. She stared at him, hypnotized. It took more than a minute for her mind to respond. When it did she was both humiliated and angered. He's treating me like some dumb kid, she told herself.

It was just enough to pull her back into herself.

"Of course," she said. "I'm a good shopper. I can go in the car. I'll call the city and have—no, that won't do. I'll have a car brought out for our use. I can drive a car." And I'm talking like a frightened child, she told herself. Get a grip on yourself, Hammond!

"Beaumont," he said, and scratched his head. "Plenty of flat places down at Beaumont. The helicopter is sitting out there behind the corral. We'll both go."

"I forget you can fly that machine," Rachel said. She ducked her head to hide the harried look that flooded her eyes. She remembered vividly her last trip in *his* chopper, and wasn't sure she was prepared for another wild ride. But he was waiting, watching, daring her to make a commitment.

"Of course," she said. "Right after breakfast. You're cooking, Charlie." He smiled at her then, a genuine, gentle smile. As both sides of his mouth curved upward, she could see a little dimple developing at his left cheek. Altogether a fine man, she told herself. Why was I in such a panic? And then she blushed at the thought. He saw that, too, and treasured it.

Both Rachel and Charlie were sitting up late after a strenuous day. "I'm beginning to feel pretty ancient," Charlie said as he put down yesterday's paper. "A full day down in the big city? Just suppose we had three or four kids along with us. They never stop saying 'why?'— or 'why not?' Why do you suppose kids talk like that?"

"It *was* nice," Rachel responded. She was sitting opposite him on the big lounger, with a mass of yarn sprawled over her feet. "And no, I haven't any idea when they stop saying those things. But I suppose I'd better give it some thought. You've had a lot of experience with children? Darn this stuff!"

"More than I'd care to recall. I can't exactly recall how many nephews and nieces I've had to deal with over the years. But then, being away in the miltary for so long, one tends to forget. What are you doing?"

"Can't you see? I'm knitting."

"Oh? I would have sworn that was one of the things you seldom did."

Her full mop of hair had fallen over her eyes. She pushed it away to look at him. "Sarcasm?"

"Sarcasm? Not from me. I don't know a thing about knitting."

In the lamplight his face had softened, and somehow she believed him. It takes a lot of doing to believe him, she told herself, but I'm going to do it regularly from now on. After all, he's done a great thing for me. I wonder why I didn't enjoy it? You don't suppose I'm one of those frigid women?

"Neither do I," she said. "But so many people knit that I figure I could learn if I applied myself to it. But——"

"But—no?"

"But no." Her mind reverted to her favorite subject. "You were away a long time?"

"Off and on," he reported. "Enough to lose track. Long enough for some of the younger ones to forget who Uncle Charlie was."

"That must have hurt?"

"Only temporarily." He chuckled at something he remembered. "Too bad. I wish I could do something to help. Say, come to think of it, Juarez Joe knits—or crochets, or something."

"That great big Indian guy? The one with all the scars? He knits?"

"Or something like that," Charlie said. "He was in my squadron in the war, and was wounded. I don't suppose you'd know, but in many military hospitals they have people come around to teach patients all sorts of things they can do while they're recuperating. In my last incarceration I had an old lady come by twice a week to teach me to hook a rug. Down home in Texas I've got me some dandy rugs."

She put her needles down and stared at him. It wasn't the idea that he might hook rugs that interested her, it was that other thought. He had been in the war and had been wounded, and that was how he learned. Wounded? A little corner of her heart responded. Without bothering about her rules of logic, Rachel Hammond said something stupid. "You were wounded?"

"A time or two," he admitted.

She drew in her breath sharply, making a hissing sort of sound. "You were wounded a time or two? Dear God! How can you be so blasé?"

"Well," he said, "I don't think He exactly had a hand in it. I went into harm's way, and got my—er—body kicked. Nothing serious. I still have all my arms and legs." He lifted up each member to illustrate. "Flying in wartime is a dangerous profession. I heartily recommend to everyone I meet that they not try it."

"But—you're a hero!"

"Not exactly." He lay his newspaper aside and gave her his full attention. "Heroes are people who give everything they have in order to save someone else. Me, I'm just a fellow who was near by when a lot of heroes did their work. But why should you worry?"

"Because I——" She barely caught herself. Because I've come to care very much about you. Because the more I see of you the more I want. Because I—because I think I'm in love with you, Charlie What's-your-name!

"And speaking of heroes and such," she said, "don't you think it's time for you to tell me what your name is?"

"Name? It's Charlie."

"Come on now, I'm not a little girl looking for lollipops. What's your last name?"

"Oh, that? Well, I was baptized Charles Albert Mathers. A common enough name, isn't it?"

"I suppose you're right." I know you're right, she told herself, but there's something strange about the name. No, not strange, unusual. What is it?

"I—there was once a Mathers family that lived in these parts. Are you related?"

"I wouldn't be surprised," he said, chuckling. "The family have always been wanderers. I don't doubt that some of their seed landed in Kansas. And Nebraska too, for that matter."

"One man by the name of Borgen," she said cautiously, "lived in Libertyville. He died a little time ago. Roger Borgen? You might know him?" She squinted, and examined his face from the side. "I know it sounds silly, but you look like him."

Charlie looked away to break her concentration. So I look like Uncle Roger? he asked himself. Hardly possible, but if true it's a real compliment. But she's only guessing. Let her keep on guessing.

"Lots of folks in our family were named Roger. Goes all the way back to the Roger Mathers who was a corsair, back in the 1600s. Hung in chains at Bristol dock, he was."

Rachel shivered and shook her head slowly. He said so much and yet didn't say so much. He'd make a great corsair, too, wouldn't he? A swashbuckler of the first water!

"I know what it is," she said. "Albert. My grandfather was named Albert. Did you ever meet him?"

"No, ma'am. I have a brother and several cousins of that name, but they're all my generation."

He's not going to admit anything, she told herself. Change the subject and try again another time! "So tell me, how were you wounded, Charlie?"

He grinned at her, that big devouring grin that swept all her suspicions away. "Not much to say about that, either," he explained. "I was flying an F-111 on an intruder mission, when half a dozen MIG 23s came up at me. Toward the end there I was zigging when I should have been zagging, and the first thing you know all the alarms went off. I think my elbow hit the ejection button, and blew my seat right out of the aircraft. Can you imagine that?"

"I can't really." But she couldn't help matching his grin. There was something about this man that tugged at her conscience. "Zigging, huh? A likely story, Charlie Mathers!"

"My grandfather always taught me, when you get your story made up, stick to it every inch," he returned. "So now, that entitles me to ask *you* a question, doesn't it?"

"Just one."

"Why the devil are you taking up all this knitting? Why the devil do you keep talking about eating for two?"

"Why..." It was hard to talk about the subject without blushing. She turned a beautiful blush red, but stuck to the course. "I'm knitting for the baby," she said. "All prospective new mothers knit. And I have to watch what I eat for the same reason."

"Perhaps I'm missing something," he drawled, his face as straight and sober as a judge.

"I don't see why. After all, you're the cause of all this."

"I am—I'm the cause of all what?"

"You know. Last night." She picked up her needles again. "But I still don't understand why I didn't enjoy some of it. All my books say that there's a—good feeling about it."

Charlie shot up out of his chair and moved a foot or two away from her. "Look, Rachel, I don't exactly know what you're talking about. Last night you were a sick little girl. I washed you off and carried you back to my bed because you didn't want to be alone. Your fever broke, and you fell asleep on my arm. It's still aching, by the way. And that, ma'am, is *all* that happened last night!"

"You mean that you—didn't?" She dropped her needles again and folded her hands in her lap. "You mean that I—that you——"

"Nothing else happened," he said firmly. "Nothing."

"Then I'm not——"

"Then you're exactly what you were before," he insisted. "I told you we'd take care of that other item when both of us were ready for it. If you think I would run around and do that to a sick woman, you're crazier than I thought you were!" With that Charlie walked out of the room, leaving Rachel huddled over herself.

God damn the man, she shouted at herself. I thought it was all over with, and it hasn't even begun. I am going to *get* that man, and I'm not going to wait around until the cows come home. I'm going to *get* that man and then throw him out on his—ear! Damn the man! Both her fists clenched. She could feel the bite of her nails as they scarred the palms of her hands. A tiny drop of moisture formed in her left eye. A moment later Rachel Hammond sat there alone and cried.

CHAPTER SIX

CHARLIE went to bed at eleven o'clock. The ranch world had changed with just a few minutes of conversation, and he was not sure he liked the change. And after Rachel had gone to bed he spent an hour or more pacing the porch.

Rachel. He pulled her out of his imagination for study. A beautiful woman, raised with a narrow need and an even narrower education. What kind of a father could the poor kid have had? A bigot, for sure, who'd then proceeded to pass the heritage on to his daughter. Her life at the ranch during these past days had been a great awakening for her. And now, he told himself, I'm sure what Uncle Roger wanted to tell me. He wanted me to take a hand with this girl and free her from all those thousand and one inhibitions and weird ideas. Like having a baby. Lord, the woman was no more than a child herself. *Why* would she want a baby?

Immediately, when he posed the question to himself, a dark cloud seemed to flow through his logic channels. A cloud bearing the picture of that evil old man hanging on the wall. Hammond, she called herself. And there was the answer. How long had her father and grandfather pounded it into her? Hammond. Rachel was the last of the line—unless she produced a baby. The only way she could be free of her ghosts was to continue the Hammond line.

And you, turkey, he told himself fiercely, you've been elected to be the proud father. Or rather, you've been

102

elected to service the poor kid, and then you're out of sight, lad!

And that, he told himself, is where I have to draw the line. There's not going to be any child of mine running around the middle of Kansas without a father. Not on your fat, ever-loving life, Rachel Hammond!

With all those thoughts in mind, it was no wonder that sleep eluded him. And when the handful of pebbles rattled off his window, all thought of rest disappeared. He struggled out of bed and padded over to the window. It opened, but only after the application of his muscle. "Joe?"

"Me, boss." The big Comanche was standing outside the window. His horse waited patiently at the end of the veranda, ground looped. "Thought I'd better ride in. There's motors runnin' down outside the fence line near Colter Springs. Trucks, I reckon. Not more'n two or three men. You comin'?"

There was no need to ask. Charlie was already pulling on his workclothes and heading for the front door.

It was difficult to walk quietly in the dark down a long wooden corridor while wearing boots, and Charlie won no prizes. So when he came along to Rachel's door it was open, and the girl was standing there in the shadows.

"What?" she whispered.

"Dunno," he responded. "Five'll get you ten it's cattle rustlers. Joe and I will ride out and investigate."

"They're my cattle."

"True. But I'm in a hurry, Rachel."

"They're my cattle. I'm coming."

In the dark he could barely see the white sheen of her nightgown. He had ridden a lot of fence lines; he had ridden with a lot of women. But never the two things at the same time.

"You mightn't be able to keep up," he groused.

"Perhaps. My cattle, my fences, and I'm coming."

"Stubborn woman!"

"You'd better believe it."

It was easier to give up than to try to argue her out of anything. He shrugged his shoulders and headed for the door. "You get dressed. Something warm. I'll go get us a couple of horses."

With Joe to help, the two horses were quickly ready. They had waited no more than two minutes when Rachel came out of the house wearing boots, blue jeans, a heavy sweater, and a wind jacket. Without a word she swung up into her saddle.

She handled her horse in true Western fashion, slouching in the saddle for the long ride, rather than stiffening her backbone. Horse and girl seemed to be welded together. Charlie gave a grunt of approval. The wind came up slightly, blotting out the noise as steel-shod hoofs hit the ground, as leather and steel chattered when they rubbed across each other. Not absolute silence, but close enough.

"Frankie, he cut through the fence and circled around," the cowboy explained as they rode stirrup to stirrup. "Looks to be twenty-five good beef critters there. A nice evening's haul."

"When we get there," Charlie ordered, "you slip across and get on the far side of the fence cut. Me, I'll stay on this side——"

"And I'll stand fast in the middle of the gap," Rachel interrupted, "and see that none of them break through."

"The hell you will," Charlie said, trying to keep his voice down. "Should have stayed at home. This is no place for a woman. I want you to—what the hell is that you've got?"

"Don't panic," she returned. "It's a .44 calibre six-shot revolver. You've never seen one before?"

"I've seen one," he growled as he kneed his horse over beside her. "I've seen one," he repeated, "in the hands of a young fool who thought he knew something, and ended up dead. Give me that thing."

"Damned if I will." Rachel swore two well-rounded oaths at him, and then squeaked as he snatched the weapon out of her hand. "Give me back that gun."

"As you say," he lectured solemnly, "damned if I will." She snatched at it, to no avail. "If you *had* to carry one out on a ride like this you certainly wouldn't have a shell under the hammer. I thought Hammond didn't raise any idiot children, but I can see I'm wrong."

"Give me that revolver," she said. Every word was accented, deliberate, reinforced by her anger.

"I said no. I mean no. We're the good guys, Rachel Hammond. Even if I gave it back to you unloaded there's no way of telling what the other side would think if they saw it. No Guns. All capital letters."

Rachel could see that he meant every word of it. Yet the Wild West movies were all she knew of rustling cattle. "Then how in the world are you going to stop them?"

"With this," he muttered. Slung on the far side of his saddle was a lariat. He uncoiled it for a moment, letting her eyes follow by moonlight as he built a loop. "Twenty feet of good, solid rope. It used to be rawhide, but today it's nylon."

"But I don't know how to make one of those things go," she wailed.

"Shush," he whispered. "We're too close already. Act like a mature woman for a change, Rachel." He was too far away for her to hit him. She would have liked to. But of all the other men Rachel Hammond knew, none would have hit her back. This fellow... There was enough of a *maybe* about him for her to kick her mount and move a safe distance away.

The men at the parked truck felt very sure of themselves. They were talking up a storm, and setting up a floodlight, as if they thought the world belonged to them. Charlie reined in and dismounted, and the others did the same.

"What the hell?" Charlie said under his breath.

"We set up a decoy camp about twelve miles that a-way," Joe returned. He gestured vaguely toward the southwest. "I learned something from the military, Major."

"Don't Major me," he said softly. "You go ahead across to the other side of their fencecut." A mournful whippoorwill cried from the far side of the fence.

"That boy never learns," Joe commented. "Makes a whippoorwill sound like a crow. But he's over there— in back of them." And with that, the Comanche slid down and disappeared in the thigh-high prairie grass.

Charlie moved over to the nearest fence post and hunkered down. Rachel came up beside him and did the same. Close enough to talk, but not close enough to touch. I'm no fool, she told herself, and if he whacks me it'll be a real whack. Besides, I want at least a hundred more answers.

"Major?"

"Just an old custom," he told her. "They called my grandfather 'General' for years, and him just a country preacher."

"General?"

"Yes, General."

"Why?"

"Damn it, Rachel Hammond, will you kindly button your lip? We aren't out here to have a social tea."

"I want to know!"

"My Gawd. If I tell you, will you shut up?"

"Yes. For the moment."

"Okay, they called him General because he was a brigadier general."

"But——"

He shut her off by putting his big palm across her mouth, and not too gently. "You promised," he hissed, "and here they come."

And here they came indeed. The two cowpokes who had ridden off with Hendrix after that big argument. One carried a big pair of wire cutters. The other stepped out of the way to avoid being hit, as the first man cut the upper strand of wire, and then the two below it. "Got to make the cut ten feet wider. Don't drag it too far," one of them murmured. "Just enough to let us bring them through. What's the matter?"

"Lost my other glove," the other man grumbled. "I better go back to the truck and get another pair. Don't wanna get all cut up on that barbed wire."

"I mighta known you'd find some excuse. The barbs on this here wire ain't hardly sharp enough to..." But his partner had gone. Mumbling to himself, the first man moved the cut strands of wire a few feet and then stepped across the fence line.

Rachel just could not keep her cool. It had been a long night, filled with bitter argument. The long ride in the cool air had added something to it all. And now, as she shifted her weight, Charlie's hand came down on the top of her head and actually pushed her down into the prairie grass. She rolled over, ready to put up a fuss.

But over her head she could hear the humming of his lariat as he ran out a loop. The cowpoke was a standing target, outlined by the searchlights. He did manage to get out one, "What the hell——?" when the loop dropped over his head.

The other end of the lariat was still attached to the pommel of Charlie's saddle. And his horse knew just as much about cutting out cattle as his rider. As soon as he felt the tension on the rope, the horse backed up. The rope tightened. The man flopped over on his back. And with the speed and practice of a rodeo rider, Charlie was on him with two pegging ropes in his hands. He might not have set a rodeo record, but it was time enough. Their prisoner, tied hand and foot, was towed back into the shadows, gagged, and retied with a fresh rope. Before Rachel could bring up word one of her protest, Charlie was back beside her, recoiling his lariat.

"Always carry two," he whispered in her ear. "This one's for throwin', the other's for tying." She started to protest. His heavy hand on her shoulder kept her locked in place. "Don't you dare move a muscle," he warned her.

There was a place for indignation, and Rachel Hammond knew that that place was not here. One man had been taken out. Two remained. And how those two were to be enticed out into the open she had no idea. So when the hand on her shoulder pushed, she relaxed flat on the ground, almost as if she were four feet down in the water, with the prairie grass weaving in the breeze high over her head. Somewhere over her head there were man noises.

"Lou? Where the hell are you, Lou?" And then, at a lower rate, almost talking to himself, "Shoulda known he'd skip out. Always avoiding the work and claiming the payoff." The noises, the mutterings, all went by them, and then she could feel Charlie come up to one knee and make that looping lariat whistle as he built up a rotation. Then another moment of silence, and an inarticulate cry from somewhere beside her, over where the cattle were bedded down. And then that sequence of sound. The whir of the rope airborne, the quick tug backward as the horse took up the slack, a jingle of spurs as Charlie went after this second man, and then a drag and a bump as another helplessly squirming body was added to their pile.

Rachel came up to her knees, a move that brought her head almost clear of the grass. Another form was slithering toward them. In the light of the searchlight she could see the tops of the grass move. Juarez Joe came up out of the grass and said noncommittally, "Don't need me at all," he murmured. "I could have stayed in my sleeping bag for all the good I've done."

"There's one more?"

"Nope. The kid got him from the backside a couple of minutes ago. It's that Hendrix fella. Now what do we do, boss?"

"Take them in to the sheriff," Rachel said excitedly. "Caught red-handed."

"If we had a tree I suspect you'd want to lynch them," Charlie said, chuckling.

"Well, why shouldn't we? They were caught rustling cattle, weren't they?"

"Have to prove it in court," he returned. "Lawyers and courtrooms and legalities. We couldn't prove a thing at the moment."

"My Lord, you don't suppose we have to turn them loose? I'll be darned if——"

"Rachel, you are surely your father's daughter. Calm down now." At that moment the younger Comanche came riding into the circle of light, a man walking in front of him. Hendrix, out of breath but too proud to accept defeat, glared at them and then hunkered down, the rope still around his shoulders.

"You ain't smart enough to make this stick," he muttered. "You might just as well turn us loose."

"Maybe you're right," Charlie agreed amiably. "We certainly couldn't prove intent if there aren't any of our cattle inside your truck." A moment of silence, and then a laugh from Hendrix.

"Well, there ain't," the man yelled at them. "You can't prove a thing."

"Probably not," Charlie admitted, as if he had not a care in the world. Both the Comanche ranch hands had disappeared. In a moment there was the sound of cattle being awakened against their will. After a few seconds they quietened down again, settled in. Twenty minutes later the two cowboys walked back into camp.

"Three head of beef in that truck," Joe reported. "All of them with our fresh brand on them. I got instant photographs of them."

"That's a damn lie," Hendrix yelled as he came clumsily to his feet. "We never laid a hand on them cows!"

"Probably not," Charlie said. "Probably they just up and climbed that ramp, looking for something good to eat."

"You can't make that stick," Hendrix muttered, but he was perspiring in the coolness of the night, and his hand was shaking.

"I don't doubt you're right," Charlie agreed. "I'll tell you what we'll do. We'll bed down out here with

his. Startled, wide-open eyes. He broke away from her
and took a deep breath.

"That ain't exactly the way it was supposed to be,"
he muttered. She managed to free one hand from around
his neck and wiped the perspiration running down off
his forehead. "What the hell are you doing to me?"

"Don't ask me," she replied wryly. "I'm the one being
punished, aren't I?"

"And you damn well better not forget that." He had
to do something to maintain his position. Be angry, he
told himself. Be mean. Be prepared to do it again! But
mind overcame emotion. He kneed his horse over beside
the mare and, almost as if she were a fifty-pound sack
instead of a one-hundred-and-twenty-pound woman,
swung her back into her own saddle.

"And now ride," he ordered. "Not like Paul Revere.
More like the US cavalry, who took their time and tried
ever to have the horses break a leg!"

"I wish I were a horse," she mused.

"What in God's name for?"

"I notice you treat all the horses in a very gentlemanly
[man]ner."

"But they deserve it."

"And I don't?"

"You could say that."

[Mar]y came fastest when summoned. Rachel had
[troub]le with her reins. Her hands were shaking too much.
[The] mare hardly knew which command to obey, and
[ended] up by doing none. "Now look what you've done,"
[he m]uttered.

["W]hat? Me?"

["Yo]u indeed," she said, touching the animal's side
[with he]r heel. The mare broke into a canter, and the

things just the way they are, and one of us will go round
up the sheriff and bring him out."

"Hah! He ain't gonna come all the way out here just
for a few cows." Hendrix, feeling things go his way for
a change, settled himself down into the grass and relaxed. "Must be more than forty miles from here to the
sheriff's office."

"Yup," Charlie replied as he got to his feet. "And
it's almost eight miles back to the house and our helicopter, so Ms. Rachel and I had better be on our way."

"Helicopter?" Hendrix yelped.

"Yup. Progress has come to the Kansas plains. And
while we're gone we'll leave you in the hands of two of
the finest Texas Indians."

"What tribe?" Hendrix gasped.

"Comanches," Charlie returned. "Unreconstructed
Comanches. You boys be sure you're good, 'cause there's
no tellin' what they might decide to do. C'mon, Rachel."

She automatically put out her hand and he pulled her
to her feet. As they walked the fence line toward their
mounts, she tugged him to a stop. "You're really not
going to leave them at the mercy of those Indians?"

"Exactly what I have in mind, lady." He pulled her
closer, until she stood chin to chin with him. Well, not
exactly that. Her chin was some six inches lower than
his. "I'd think by now, Ms. Rachel, that you wouldn't
be so quick to judge people. Juarez Joe is a graduate of
Texas Aggie. My family actually owns six ranches down
in the Panhandle. Joe is the general manager of the corporation that runs them all. He's come all the way up
here just to do me a favor. And the kid is his oldest
son."

"Well, I never——" she started to say, when he lost
his temper.

"No, you never do," he snapped as he swung her up in his arms. "Never think, that is. Do you know what your trouble is?"

"I—no, and I don't want to hear," she said.

"I'm damn sure you don't," he told her as he stalked over to the horses. "Spoiled damn brat. You seem to think that nobody else but you has any rights. You'd do better if you could run this ranch with robots. Then you could put them away in the barn with the horses every night and forget about them." He set her down none too gently at the side of her mare. "And now, lady, if you could condescend to put a foot in the stirrup?"

He didn't wait for her quiescence. He picked her up again, hands around her waist, and forcibly thrust her left foot into the deep stirrup. Before he could think of anything else, she told herself, I'd better move!

Her graceful body swung up, but so full of fear was she that she almost went over the mare's back and down the other side. Almost, but not quite. He still had a hand at her waist. The horse was hardly three years old, and not accustomed to all the excitement. She sidled away from him, pranced a step or two, and then responded to the spurs and was off into the darkness.

"Damn fool woman," he muttered as he mounted up and went on after her.

"Look at them go," Joe commented to his son. "Crazy disease, love. Don't catch it."

"You needn't worry," the kid returned. "I'm immune. Had it six times already."

"And only nineteen," his father groaned. "Listen to them go. Any minute now, one of those animals is gonna put a foot in a pothole and they'll end up ass over teakettle. C'mon, boy, let's get us some shut-eye."

It took just that amount of time for Charlie to up with Rachel. He grabbed at a rein and pulled mounts to a walk. "I didn't say break your neck, growled at her.

"Keep away from me. If I had my way," she y at him, "I'd——"

"Didn't your father or mother ever spank you?' interrupted.

Her mare danced around in a circle, fighting his on the reins. His own animal, like any good qua horse, moved with the mare, always keeping his he her direction.

"No!" she half screamed at him. "And don't you're going to do anything of that kind."

"Not me," he said gruffly. "You're far too that. But believe me, I've got to do somethir hand on the mare's reins forced that animal to side by side with his own. He dropped the re over in her direction, and swept her out of t

"Don't you dare!" she roared.

"Oh, I dare." It started out to be a punis not more than a second after his lips touc thought of punishing flew out of his head lips, stiff when first he touched them, b laxing under his probe. A moment of c blocked access to her mouth, and then th down under the assault of his tongue. 7 was gentle. His arms tightened around he felt their pressure as Rachel Hammond the first time in all her almost-thirty ye and threw her arms around his neck as her way deeper into his grasp. She h when the attack began. Now she open into his, so close and so commandir

gelding joined just alongside. "I just don't understand you," she said reflectively. "We took so much care."

"We?"

"My two doctors and I. You have no idea what trouble we went to just so that everything would be perfect."

"And I've failed? I'm not perfect."

"Well, that's one of the problems," she said. "You're better than perfect. And then on the other hand, not so good at all. You just don't meet my ideal. I guess that's what I want to say."

"I'm sorry to hear you say that, but an honest opinion is the best thing in the world. And how about you?"

"Me? There never was any attempt to measure me. I am what I am. There's no possibility that I'll change."

"What a shame," he retorted. "Somebody should have measured you a long time ago. Somebody should have taken you in hand and got your engine running straight."

"And you're that somebody?"

"I could have been." He pulled over his Stetson and wiped his brow. "I could have been, but your crazy needs got me to staggering around the hay barn. What is it that you want? To continue the Hammond dynasty?"

"I'll admit that. My father left no doubt that he wanted a boy. When he lost little Jimmy he went full speed ahead to make me *think* like a man, even though he thought there were lots of man-things I couldn't do. So yes, this child I want is to serve my father's memory. And——" She broke off, turning her head into the wind. There were a multitude of things she wanted to tell him, but did not dare.

"And?"

"And I don't think any of that is important to you. Leave it."

"Not if you want me to be this boy's father. It has to be a boy, I suppose."

"Of course," she said bitterly. "I'd hate to think about having a girl, and then having to do it all over again." Another moment of silence as the horses continued their steady lope toward the house. "Well, in any case, it shouldn't bother you. Obviously you're not up to doing it. After we settle this business with the rustlers, I think I'll go back to town and take up with the magazine until we can find a better candidate than you."

"And what happens to me?"

"Just write it down as an experiment that didn't work. You might, if you wouldn't mind, look around and find me another foreman. Unless you might consider staying on yourself?"

"No. There's no way I could just hang around. Once we leave, the party's over, Ms. Rachel. I suppose I could find you a foreman without any trouble. Unemployment is way up, all over Kansas, Nebraska, Wyoming. I'll put out the word. And in the meantime, Joe could look after things for you."

"And you, Charlie? What will you do?"

"The things I came up to Kansas to do, I guess. I have to take over my uncle's place, execute his will—things like that. He had no children. I'll bet things are all run down. My uncle was an invalid for the last six months of his life. Things can go to pot under a hand that's bedridden for that length of time."

"I can see that. I have to thank you, Mr. Mathers. You've taken hold and made some marvelous improvements in the ranch. Absentee ownership isn't something that makes the cows grow, is it?"

They had just turned into the yard, and approached the silent helicopter, its rotor blades turned the length

of the fuselage and lashed down, chocks under the wheels
to keep it from rolling, lines pegged out fore-and-aft to
secure against the wind.

They drew rein beside the beautiful white machine,
and he swung out of the saddle. "Want to come with
me?"

"I—don't think so," she said cautiously as she stepped
down from her mount. "I think we've said everything
that needs to be said."

"Well, not quite," he said as he walked around his
mount and came to her side. "There's probably a million
things that ought to be said. Like, for instance, you're
one hell of a lady, Hammond. But after all this work
you've put into this baby proposition, you're just going
to give it all up?" She backed away from him, as if he
were a lit stick of dynamite. His voice rose, and he gave
her a little shake. "You're just going to walk away at
the first real obstacle? You really didn't mean it, after
all, did you?"

"I meant it," she cried indignantly. "I haven't given
up the project, I've just given up on you! I'll find a way,
believe me. And another man, if need be." Her voice
fell to a whisper as she ducked her head. He must *not*
see her crying!

He put his hands on her shoulders, and looked down
at her. In the darkness she could no longer read his face.
"I wish it could end differently," he said. There was a
shadowed sound in his voice, real regret. She shivered.
"Like—oh, hell."

He snatched her up in his arms again and gently, pos-
sessively held her. It's not something I really want, she
lied to herself. He's not going to dominate me and turn
me into a house mother with ten kids. I'm fully in
command of my own needs and wants, and there's no

way he can take me over and try to remodel me. Some
cowpoke from Texas? The ony thing going for him is
that he *does* take a bath every day. And for the rest of
it, I can do without him.

That was all thought out *before* he kissed her. Afterward she had no real memory of what went on when
his lips sealed her off from the world. Riots of colored
fireworks seemed to be shooting off, high in the sky. But
not so high that she wasn't still higher. She flew among
the wispy clouds, looking down at the green and gold
and red of the rockets, played against the silver and white
of the fields, all bathed in the rays of a weak little moon.

Her body shivered from head to toe. There was no
control she could institute against the feeling, so finally
she just lay back against his arms and let it all happen.

Somehow it ended. Somehow she found herself still
six inches or more above ground. He let her down,
regrettably. The arches of her feet seemed to have difficulty accepting the reality of weight. But by then it was
done. His hug lasted a moment longer, a moment to
savour as she leaned her face against his shoulder. His
hand came up and riffled through her hair, almost as if
he were giving a benediction.

"Goodbye, Hammond." Softly said, with a definite
tinge of regret.

"I won't see you again?"

"No reason to, lots of reasons why not. No, I'll get
the sheriff's men out to the camp, take care of all the
paperwork. What you ought to do is get a good night's
sleep and then get back to your magazine. Right?"

"I guess," she said, and then shivered as she squared
her shoulders. Rachel Hammond had disappeared. Now
it was just plain Hammond. "Come by the office some
time, and I'll pay you off."

"No need," he assured her. "I didn't do anything. There's no need to pay me off. We'll just call it quits, shall we?"

Yes, she told herself as she backed off a few feet. We'll just call it quits. Why should it hurt so much? She tried one of her father's prescriptions. Straighten up, freeze all your muscles in position, adopt a glare—even though he can't really see it in the fading light of the setting moon. Do it, Hammond. Don't ever let this man see you're crying, because if you do he'll think it's just a farce we're playing!

In the gathering darkness he could barely see her hand waving slowly.

He turned and went over to the chopper. Habit led him to unfasten the lines, pull the chocks, make his walk-around inspection. Training took him into the pilot's seat to complete his engine start-up and the electrical tests. Memory held him as the rotors turned gently. Memories of what might have been. At which point he shook himself like an old sheepdog and did his best to force her out of his mind. He turned on his navigational lights, revved up the engine, and the lovely white chopper set itself and vaulted into the sky, marking its movement only by the red marker lights on the fuselage.

Memories. A wonderful, bitter, maladjusted woman, who needs a man like me to marry up with. But she doesn't want to marry. A child would be nice, but not its father. What kind of a racket is that? He shook his head again. The flight instruments glowed blue and green at him. The altimeter said two hundred feet. He set the controls to "hover," turned on the radio, and went about contacting the sheriff's department.

CHAPTER SEVEN

RACHEL HAMMOND looked around her pyramid office and sighed in disgust. Everything that she had seen since that day of her return from the ranch left her with a dyspeptic stomach.

"Look, Elmer," she said, trying to hold her voice in control. "I've gone over every issue you've put out since I left. They all feature the same subject."

"What's that, Hammond?" Elmer Chatmas had been editor of the magazine since her grandfather's day. He knew a thing or two—or three.

"Boredom," she screamed at him. "Plain out-and-out boredom. Do you realize that our circulation has dropped eight thousand in the weeks I've been away?"

"Holidays," he said. "Summertime. People are out of town. Our kind of readers don't take the *Gossiper* along with them for summer beach parties. We're not the *Digest*, you know."

"I know that," she snapped. "But still the front page is filled with boredom!"

"See," he gloated. "Just what I told you. You've been away just a couple of weeks and you've come back loaded for bear. What do we do next?"

"I'll tell you what we're going to do," she insisted. "We're going to prove to all the world that the *National Gossiper* has still got a sting in its tail. Now, for next week, I want you to tear down whoever we have for the front page, and run up as big a campaign against him as possible. The works. Theft, women, May and December relationships——"

"Embezzlement," Elmer interrupted. "That always goes over well!" The idea caught her fancy.

"Yeah. That's just it. As big a balloon as we can run. Why in the world didn't I think of embezzlers before? Our readers always go for the money bit. Who got what, that sort of thing."

"Because, love, your mind doesn't run in those channels. You're really a very nice girl." Elmer needed a smoke screen. He defied all the office rules by pulling out his pipe and lighting up.

He must have commented along those critical lines for the past three years, and always received a mild reaction. But this time she blew her skull. "Nice?" she roared. "I'll give you nice! I want this next issue to be so raw that *nice* never ever comes to mind when he— when they think of us."

Elmer almost choked over his pipe. "You mean— rotten?"

"I mean rotten!"

"No matter who it is?"

"I don't give a damn if it's the Archbishop of Chicago." And then a quavering pause, and a question. "It isn't the Archbishop, is it?"

"No, but——"

"Don't tell me. I don't want to know. Next Monday I want to open the paper and be so thoroughly surprised that I'll think it's a good run no matter what the story is. Make it big. It's going to be the last gossip issue that we ever run. After this we're reorganising into something more literary. I'm tired of being known as the queen of smut. Got it?"

"You mean that? You don't want any sort of a hand in the production of the magazine for next week, and you want it to be as rotten as possible?"

"That's exactly right."

He got up clumsily. Sixty-five was a difficult age. Knees no longer bent on command. Elbows had a tendency to jam up. Minds had a tendency to cloud over. Make it as rotten as possible? That wasn't hard to do, but the little lady was going to be shocked all the way down to her shoe inserts. And like a Hammond she would have to bear up under the shock, even if it killed her. Elmer Chatmas headed for the door. "And what are you going to be doing as I create this—spectacular magazine?"

"Getting ready for the changeover. The first thing we need to do is streamline. We won't be making much of a profit for the first six months. I'm going to start an investigation," she told him, a fierce grin on her face. "Haven't you noticed that every time you see a figure around this office, it's always rounded off? Our circulation is 630,000? Come on, now, exactly that, or do we throw away a bushel of other, real figures instead of all those zeros?

"I get payroll accounts twice a month. Always they come out in nice round figures. Nobody ever enters dimes and quarters and nickels, and I'll bet there are a tremendous number of them!

"Every time we do a big story, all the victims come out in round numbers! And all the detectives are heroes. Well, let me tell you something, Elmer! This month will put an end to all that. I'm going to go through every department in this building and shake it by the neck until it gets away from round numbers!"

"Yes, well." Elmer sucked on his pipe, and then let it go out. "Don't overdo it," he told her. "You and I, we can't put out this magazine all by ourselves, you know. Push a few people too far and they'll up and revolt, my dear."

"If they do, that's my business!"

"As you say. If they do, that's your—business." He closed the door and was gone before she could add to her last statement. Who was it on that ranch? he mused. Somebody got to our Hammond, and left her on half-cock, ready to fire at a moment's notice.

Rachel walked over to the window and looked out down Main Street. Traffic was slow, with reason. Two blocks away on Eisenhower Avenue a bus and a truck had run into each other. A police helicopter came in out of the smog from the west, and circled the site.

The craft's appearance jolted her heart. *He* flew a machine like that. A chopper. And she hadn't seen or heard from him in a week. Not since he had crammed himself into his machine and flown out of the Bar Nine ranch.

Rachel had come back to town more sedately, in her limousine. She intended to avoid helicopter rides for a lifetime—or maybe two lifetimes. She had caught her heel on the rug as she tried to get out of the car. It was just the time and place for Charlie to be there to catch her, she'd told herself. But he wasn't, and her chauffeur had had to do the catching.

Still fuming, Rachel had rushed into the pyramid building, doing her best to avoid the tears.

"You need a handkerchief?" her secretary had asked, and had her head bitten off. The word had quickly spread that Hammond was back, and in no good spirits. The rest of the staff had made themselves hard to locate until the boss went off to her apartment at the Sheridan.

Where, alone in her apartment, with the doors closed and locked, she had thrown herself on the massive bed and had a good cry.

Charlie Mathers made intermittent trips back to the ranch for the next three days, to set things up. Two new, young hands, well recommended, had appeared on the scene, as well as a foreman, an elderly, retired master sergeant from the brown-shoe army and Fort Riley. And a promise from Juarez Joe and his son to "hang around in the neighborhood until they get their feet on the ground." Then, shaking the dirt of the Flint Hills from his boots, Charlie took his helicopter back to Beaumont and rented a car for the trip to Libertyville.

"Just what in hell are you up to?" Frank Losen, Charlie's lawyer, threw himself down into the depths of the supersofa, and twisted to pick up his glass. "You've had yourself a nice vacation. I don't know anything you'd like more than a chance to run a ranch."

"Bull feathers," Charlie snorted. "Good time? With Holy Rachel at hand? Good Lord, that woman could convince you without any trouble that the sun rises in the west!"

"Oh? It doesn't? Lord, this is lousy Scotch. Where the devil did you get it?"

"Where else? Across the line in Missouri. You know they have drinking laws in Kansas. Drink it and start talking. What have you learned?"

Losen pulled a sheaf of papers out of his briefcase. He shuffled a couple of them to the top of the pile. "Now, then. It's all one corporation, Hammond-Borgen, with two divisions. One is the magazine, the other is the ranch. Over the last fifteen years the ranch hasn't made a penny."

"So the magazine supports everything?"

"That's the story. Now, your grandpa held fifteen percent of the whole shebang, but when Rachel's father took the magazine into pornography——"

"Pornography?"

"Well, that's what your grandpa called it."

"So he sold all his stock?"

"Lord, no. He loved the ranch, and he wasn't about to separate from it. He just—well, he just segregated the stock, took his name off the company books, and put his shares into a blind trust. He made believe that the magazine just didn't exist!"

"I—wait a minute. What are you telling me?"

His lawyer laughed at him. "What I'm telling you is that you have just inherited forty percent of the Hammond-Borgen Corporation from your uncle Roger."

"And Grandpa has another fifteen per cent in some kind of a trust? Do I understand all this? If I could get the old coot to vote with me, we could take over the entire corporation! Throw the rascals out, so to speak? But he wouldn't, would he? He wouldn't be caught dead having anything to say, good or bad, about that rag!"

"Never a chance," Frank retorted. "He wouldn't! You know your grandfather is as straitlaced as they come. No, dear friend, if you have some hanky-panky planned, you have to make up to the trustee who controls the blind trust."

"Who is?"

"Is this really the best Scotch you have?"

Charlie walked over to the head of the sofa. "I'd better warn you, Frank, I'm not in any cheerful mood!" He paused for a moment, rubbing his chin. "Frank—yes,

I have a bottle of Chivas Regal, forty years old. I could probably remember where I put it. Maybe I—no, I'm sure it's here somewhere."

"I'd kill for a drink like that. Your grandpa thought I was an up-and-coming young man, a real churchgoer. 'Set your mind to run this magazine straight and decent,' he told me."

"Frank, don't try my patience!"

"Of course not. I'm your grandpa's trustee."

"Ah. That bottle is upstairs in my bedroom. And I believe I'll join you." He was back in minutes, waving two bottles in the air, rather than one.

"Before we begin the festivities," Frank Losen said very seriously, "the only thing you could do, holding the majority of the stock, would be to vote her out of office."

"I know that."

"Then be sure you know that being the boss of that corporation is all she lives for. Throw her out on the street and she'll crack up for sure."

"Yes, and I know that too," Charlie said. And then a pause for consideration. Rachel Hammond, broken into little pieces? All that beauty smashed? Good Lord! "Come on, pull the cork out of that thing and let's get down to some serious drinking."

So, what with the morning after, and a multitude of little things that needed to be done in his own office, it was Monday morning before he took to the streets of Libertyville to wander, restore his memories, and think what next he might do about Rachel Hammond. He had long since given up the option to do nothing.

He didn't need a great deal of planning. His lawyer caught up with him shortly after twelve o'clock in the

Barbecued Beef, a downtown restaurant of strange repute.

"You're going to eat in this place?"

"You bet. I can see you're in good humor today."

"But—they keep half the light bulbs unscrewed so you can't see what you're eating. The salad's made in downtown Hamtramck by a bunch of laid-off auto workers!"

"You've got the wrong idea, Frank. If you come out for salad, go to a salad place. This place serves beef. It's the best beef in the world, my friend. And when they cook it they do a minimum amount of damage to the thing, and all you have to do is cut it—with a fork, mind you—and chew it down. Now, did you come to ruin my lunch, or do you have something else on your so-called mind?"

"I came to invite you out to the ball game. Kansas City is playing at home this afternoon. We could hop over in that little chopper of yours, see the game, and then explore the Kansas City nightlife."

"Well, that's very kind——"

"But I'm not going to, man. Coming in the door, I spotted a copy of the *National Gossiper*, and all hell broke loose."

"What do you mean?"

"Here. Take a look." He passed the magazine over, upsetting Charlie's coffee cup.

"Look, I don't have time for magazine studies. I've finally made up my mind about this Hammond lady. Too much pussyfooting's been going on in these parts. I'm going over to lay it straight on the line."

"You'd better look first, buddy."

"One thing at a time," Charlie said. "I'm not smart enough to look in two directions at the same time."

"So you're going to track down Hammond, and you're going to tell her something. What?"

"I'm going to tell her we're going to get married. And that's all there is to that!" Charlie pushed his chair back and tipped a salute to his lawyer and went out into the sunshine on Custer Avenue. Frank remained at the table and watched as his client stepped out smartly into the sunshine.

"Sure. Get married," Frank muttered. "Then you'll need two lawyers. Or maybe three!"

"What I need before I see this woman is somebody to hit," Charlie muttered as he came opposite the *Gossiper* building. "Somebody big."

"Hot damn!" The exclamation came because those two big bodyguards were still standing at the downstairs door of the *Gossiper*, just as they had been not three weeks ago. Male! Big! Hittable!

"Gentlemen. Are you employees of this magazine?"

"We are. Haven't we seen you somewhere before?"

"Have you read this rag today?"

"Who, me? I wouldn't touch it with a ten-foot pole."

"Me neither," the other guard said. "Lousy. Full of lies, innuendo, all that stuff. I don't know what keeps them out of jail for so long."

"Oh, Lord," Charlie grumbled. He smacked one fist into the other palm. How in the world can you beat up someone who agrees completely with what you have to say? "Excuse me," he said as he walked around them to go in.

"Hey, you can't go in there. The place is closed. And I understand Hammond has hired a couple of extra guards."

"I just hate to do this," Charlie chortled, "but I'm going in. Are you stopping me?"

"I'm stopping you."

"Wait just a minute," the second guard said. "Haven't we played this song before—with this same guy?"

"Come on, stop me," Charlie insisted.

The two guards stared at each other for a second. They must have had a corporate communication system in their heads. They both turned to Charlie. "Stop you? Not a chance. If you want to go in, mister, you just go right ahead."

"Damn," Charlie said. He rocked back and forth on the balls of his feet. "Won't change your minds?"

They shook their heads. Charlie shook his too, then reached forward to open the door. A helping hand was there before him. "You just go right ahead." A second later they added, "Sir." The two of them managed a little bow and stepped out of the way.

Disgusted, Charlie erupted into the ground-floor lobby like a tornado looking for a place to touch down. There was not a soul in sight. An elevator door hissed at him and opened. Still pounding his hands together, he moved into the elevator and scanned the directory. Every office had a name, and he knew none of them. But finally there was one discreet little button labeled "Penthouse." He pushed it so hard that the machinery shuddered before it shut its door and started upward.

It was a slow elevator, which gave Charlie Mathers plenty of time to organise his "mad" and get it steamed up. The lights blinked at him, one floor at a time. When he had counted ten, the machine he was riding stumbled to a stop, then hitched upward another inch or two before it opened its door.

He was facing a blank wall, and a closed glass door. The title on the door was just what he had expected. "Hammond," it said. "Damn woman," he muttered as he palmed the knob. The door slammed back on its stops. A woman at the desk facing him gave a little squeak of alarm, and pressed the little red button on her desk.

"You needn't squeal," Charlie said calmly. "I never eat blondes before supper. Where's Hammond?"

"She's—not here."

"And you go to church every Sunday?"

"I—you think I'm lying?"

"I know you're lying. Where's Hammond?"

"She's not here. They left just a few minutes ago."

"*They* left?"

"His name is Olsen. He won a contest. That's all I know!"

By God, Charlie told himself, another contest winner. I didn't work out, so she's got someone else to take my place! And I'm jealous as hell, that's what I am. I could kill both of them, and that's for sure.

"They've gone out to the ranch?"

The middle-aged woman before him looked petrified. "N-no," she stammered. "Hammond would never go back out there. Something happened on her last visit and she swore she would never go back there. Never!"

"Yeah," he snapped. "That I'll believe the next time a week comes up with two Tuesdays."

The elevator doors out in the hall whooshed open, and a pair of very large-looking young men fought each other to get out into the corridor. A moment later the office door opened, and they came into the office one at a time.

"What's wrong, Ms. Sally?" The bigger of the two looked as if he might be two hundred and fifty pounds, and stand six feet five. The little fellow was more likely one hundred and ninety-five, and six foot even. The woman at the desk had pushed her chair back and stood up.

"This—er—gentleman was just leaving," she said.

Charlie took another look at the pair of them, and considered. I could, he told himself, take either one of them without any trouble. I could probably take both of them—well, make that a seventy percent chance. On the other hand, since I was just going anyway—what the hey!

"Like the lady says," he agreed amiably, "I was just leaving. Excuse me?" He stepped around the pair of them gingerly, doing his best to avoid touching either of them. Safely out in the corridor, with them forming a wall between him and the secretary, he called, "You won't forget to tell Ms. Rachel that I called? And that I was very perturbed about the last issue of the magazine? And that I'll see her in court very very quickly?"

The elevator door was still open, waiting restlessly for a patron. He pushed the lobby button, the machine activated itself with a groan, and the double door swung shut. None of the three he left behind offered a comment of any kind.

The machine disgorged him in the silent lobby. Across on the other wall was a bank of pay telephones. How did you go about finding the big boss's address when she didn't want to be found? He grinned as he thumbed through the directory for the personnel office of the corporation, then dropped in his coin and dialed.

"And you're who?" the elderly lady at the other end demanded.

"William Two Feather," Charlie said. "I'm Mrs. Colchester's son. My mother is very ill, and as a former employee of your firm—they've canceled her medical insurance. Would you believe that? Forty years working for the Hammonds and they canceled her medical insurance. So I have to get in touch with Hammond, and I forgot where she's living in the city. Some hotel, I believe.''

There was a moment of silence as the clerk on the other end of the line consulted her computer. "Yes, Mrs. Colchester. Forty years service and Hammond just——''

"Turned her out of house and home. Can you beat that?'' Charlie slapped a big paw over the telephone transmitter. He had almost said, "turned her out into the snow''—it seldom snowed in Kansas in August. He was beginning to like his part too well, but there was no room for humor.

"A shame,'' the voice from Personnel said. "It's against company policy to give out any information on Hammond, but I see that Mrs. Colchester——''

"My mother,'' Charlie said mournfully.

"Yes, your mother, Mr. Two Feather. She formerly lived in the penthouse suite at the Sheridan Hotel, on Broad Street. You can find the place?''

"Easy,'' Charlie said. "Easy. I thank you. My mother thanks you. The entire Potowotami Nation thanks you.'' He dropped the handset before the clerk could gather her wits, and was out on the street in a hurry. The two door guards kept a respectable distance.

"Missed Ms. Hammond,'' one of them called after him. "She just went out the back way when you came in.''

"Thank you,'' he yelled as he dived into his rented sports car and started the engine. "There,'' he lectured himself, "all done with smoke and mirrors, and not a

fist laid on anyone. Diplomacy, that's what! The way
of the future." He was whistling as he drove off.

The Sheridan was one of the new residential hotels on
the outskirts of the city. Set back in its own enclave of
fences and trees, and discreetly guarded against all
comers, it boasted valet parking. Charlie left his prize
vehicle in the hands of the attendants and rushed into
the lobby.

"I have an emergency message for Ms. Hammond,"
he announced to the desk man. "Can I go up?"

The desk clerk looked him up and down. In the heat
of the day Charlie had abandoned his suit coat and tie,
unbuttoned the top three buttons of his shirt, and had
rolled his sleeves up above his elbows. Obviously the desk
man thought him to be not quite the type to be admitted.

"Not without authorization," the haughty clerk retorted. "I'll call and see. Your name is?"

"Mathers," he said. "Charlie Mathers."

It took but a moment for the connection to be made.
The telephone buzzed once and was picked up at the far
end. The clerk handed him the phone. With one set of
fingers crossed, he used the others to push down the
plunger, thus disconnecting the line.

"Hello," he said into the dead handset. "Rachel, this
is Charlie. Yes, Charlie Mathers. I have that information you wanted. Yes, come up right away?"

He dropped the handset back on its cradle. "She says
'come up right away,'" he told the house clerk. "Which
way?"

The clerk's face looked curdled, his lips pinched in,
as if what he had to say tasted bad. He still believed that
Charlie Mathers could not possibly be welcome in any
of the suites of *his* hotel, but the customer was always
right.

"The elevator in the corner," he said. "It's an express directly to the penthouse." He gestured toward the line of elevators in the far wall. "Car number one, the penthouse," he murmured, and then brushed his jacket off with both hands, as if he had been dealing with something undesirable.

"Pontius Pilate," Charlie said, grinning at him. "You know, wash the hands after anything as disagreeable as all that. Thank you."

The clerk fumbled for something to say, but by the time Charlie reached the elevator all he could muster was a cold, "Thank you."

This elevator knew its business. Its door closed without slamming, and it zoomed upward at high speed. Charlie, standing in the middle of the car, reached desperately for one of the wall-mounted brackets. The thing stopped the same way it had started. With enthusiasm. And the door opened on a dimly lit green corridor. There was only one door in sight.

The doorbell could be heard. Discreetly heard, of course. The door opened without a single noise. A hotel maid shrugged her shoulders at him, as if waiting for him to display his card from the plumbers' union. She sniffed at him and elevated her nose.

"And me too," he said sincerely. "I'm Charlie Mathers. Is Hammond here?"

"In the living room, but she has company already."

"I know. I think I need to see them both."

"Then I'm supposed to announce you." The little maid walked down an interior corridor ahead of him. A pair of double doors were closed. She knocked briefly, opened one door, and said, "Mr.—er—Charlie Mathers is here, ma'am!"

There was a squeal of rage from inside. The maid gestured Charlie in through the door, and then shut it behind him. She had obviously been working for Hammond long enough to know when to get out of the range of fire.

Charlie leaned back against the closed doors. In front of him, in the sunken living room, there wasn't an ounce of joy.

Rachel Hammond was rising from a pouffe at one side of the room. Across the low coffee table from her was a large young man, who looked to be one of those people who could easily win the Mr. America titles. He was dressed in blue shorts and a gray T-shirt, and evidently had spent a long time cultivating his tan and his muscles. His hair was cut short, a butch cut, shaved closely on all sides. His face was square-set, with a bulging neck. Altogether, Charlie thought, the kind of nice young man I wouldn't care to meet too often. Except for today.

Rachel, on the other hand, appeared as if she had just come out of the shower. Her hair glistened. The lace collar of her négligé was belted firmly under her white robe. The robe was buttoned up, from neck to hem, which stirred briefly about four inches below her knees. She was also wearing a face he remembered, fully flushed with anger, eyes piercing him like daggers.

"I thought I made it plain," she said firmly. "Our business venture is concluded. I have hired this gentleman to take your place. Edward, would you please...?"

The "nice young man" stepped around the coffee table, looking altogether too eager to do whatever was required. Charlie watched him move—slowly for such a well-built young man.

"Rachel, I don't think you ought to do this," Charlie temporized.

Hammond looked as if she didn't agree. Edward paused to look over his shoulder for confirmation. "Get rid of him," she snapped. He began to move forward again.

This is just what I need, Rachel told herself. The trouble with all this anguish is that it hasn't had a firm conclusion. Edward will surely destroy this—this—— She fumbled for words. Plain, honest Charlie. Not by any means the handsome young stud she had wanted, and yet he was—damn it, why do I whiffle about him? "Get to it, Edward," she repeated harshly.

And then her eyes widened and she took a couple of protective steps backward. Her nice young man had advanced up the two stair levels to where Charlie stood, and then, for some reason that Rachel could not quite see, he had fallen down. "Edward!" she yelled.

The nice young man struggled to his feet and rubbed his stomach as if it hurt. He looked around over his shoulder again, and Rachel offered him an encouraging smile. He turned back toward Charlie, made some slight motion, and fell down again!

"You know, Rachel," Charlie said, "this poor young man is liable to get hurt. In fact, I think he's already hurt. Poor kid."

"What are you doing?" she gasped. "You——"

"Exactly," Charlie said. "You sent a boy to do a man's job. And now look what we've done. I had to hit him on the jaw. I think I've broken a knuckle here. And it's all your fault. Going to get up again, son?"

Edward mumbled a word or two. There was something wrong with his jaw. "I know," Charlie said compassionately. "Women! They go through this routine all the time, looking for the 'parfit gentil knight' to slay a dragon for them. Especially this one. Here, let me help you up."

Edward cautiously accepted the offered hand, and mumbled something again.

"Yes, I know," Charlie said. "Look, the plain fact of it is she's trying to make me jealous. I have the job—a firm contract. And all you can get is trouble by scabbing. Say, look. Take a cab over to the hospital and let them fix you up. Everything is on the house. The Hammond-Borgen Corporation. Hammond here will call ahead and okay the bills. Right?" He turned around and glared at Hammond, who had suddenly become Rachel again.

"I—yes," Rachel muttered as she circled around the room, keeping at the farthest distance she could from him, and found the telephone. Meanwhile, Charlie slipped an arm around the young man and helped him out of the door.

The maid was huddled in a corner, eavesdropping and enjoying it all. "See that he gets downstairs," Charlie ordered. "And he'll need a cab to take him to the hospital." After which he left the pair of them, went back into the living room where Rachel waited, and closed the door behind him.

CHAPTER EIGHT

"WELL," Charlie said as he wiped his hands. "That certainly made me feel better."

"Barbarian," Rachel muttered as she tried to squirm farther away from him, into the depths of her couch. "You could have hurt the boy."

Charlie laughed. "Why don't you listen to what you're saying?" he asked. "Boy indeed. But old enough for your purposes? I think I hurt my knuckles more than his jaw."

"I don't care to talk about it. Violence appalls me. Please go, before I call the police."

"Ah. What a good idea. Why don't you call them? They're probably looking for you anyway." He took a quick, jerky pace up and down in front of her. "You don't abhor violence, Hammond. You abhor *physical* violence. The world is full of other kinds. I'm surprised you don't recognize that. You've suffered more mental violence than most anyone else I know!"

She came to her feet with a startled look on her face. "Don't you start now on my father. He was a good man, for all his little faults."

"Little faults? My Gawd, woman, what do I have to do to make you see the light? Well, the police will be along soon enough."

"Looking for me? I didn't do anything." Indignation fits her, he told himself. Just that little bit of color to her cheeks makes all the difference between austerity and beauty.

138

"That may be, lady, but *somebody* did *something* with that so-called magazine of yours. You'll be happy to know that we've taken out an injunction against you and your dirty rag, and I don't doubt that my lawyer has arranged for a dozen or more cops to find you and serve the writ. You certainly blew your top this time, lady."

"I don't know what you mean. I haven't seen today's issue yet." She drew that haughty cloak of the imperial Hammonds around her, swathing herself as if she were the Statue of Justice on top of the capital building. And that too, he told himself, is something we've got to settle some time soon. But that's not first priority.

"I haven't seen today's issue yet either," he assured her. "But my lawyer tells me that it's bad, even for you. Tell me, why did you bring in the boy?"

"You know why," she said bitterly. "Just because you reneged doesn't change anything. I still wanted that baby. Time is running out for me, and I can't do it all by myself. If I could I would, believe me. You don't know anyone who hates men worse than I do."

"Tell me," he said, and chuckled. "Did the boy go along with your proposal for an *in vitro* fertilization?"

"Of course he did," she snapped. "I raised the offer to four thousand dollars."

"That's certainly a good price," he agreed. "But the terms? Yetch!"

"I'll get it done, Mr. know-it-all, in spite of you and your friends. I *will* get it done. I need this child!"

"*You* need the baby, or is it your father who needed the baby? And him dead and gone these three years or more."

"Damn you. You think you know everything, don't you?"

"No, I'm far from knowing everything, Rachel. All I know is that you're frozen inside that shell of ice you've grown, and headed hell-for-leather down the road to Hades!"

"If that's my final destination," she flung at him, "at least the ice will be melted by the time I get there. Why are you badgering me? Your part in my troubles is over and done with. Did you want your money? Is that why you came?"

"For that piddling amount? Come on, Rachel, you know me better that that!"

The goading succeeded. She launched herself across the room at him, both hands extended like claws, the red gleam of her nail polish threatening death and destruction. "I'm going to——" she gabbled, and then lost control of her voice.

Charlie was no fool. He knew how dangerous claws could be. He stood still until she was almost within range, and then his longer arms snatched her wrists out of the air and pinned them to her sides.

Rachel made a couple of attempts to break loose, and then her strength failed her. For a moment she wavered back and forth, and then she bent over past her point of balance and collapsed.

Before she could hit the floor he caught her, and cuddled her, sobbing, against his chest. He carried her over to one of the overstuffed chairs, and sat down, holding her in his lap.

"There, now, Rachel," he coaxed. "Cry it all out."

She tried to struggle on, but had not the strength. The tears flowed like rivers. She ducked her head into the softness of his shirt and cried her years of anger away. Poured out her anguish on to shoulders broader and stronger than her own.

Charlie Mathers was not the world's greatest planner. The crying he had hoped for, but once it started he ran out of ways to guide it. Psychology I and II had been part of his freshman education, and a good many rivers have gone over a good many dams since that time. Not knowing what to do next, he shifted her weight, ran one hand through the tangle of her hair, and hoped for the best. But the softness of her, lying there in his lap, introduced thoughts once held in thrall by his anger. Controls he had thought to be imbedded in steel suddenly turned to jelly. His suddenly clumsy fingers tugged at the two top buttons of her robe, and brushed it open. Without any particular instruction, his hand slid down into the opening, touched and cupped her breast, and gradually massaged its tip.

The woman stopped crying. "What are you doing?" she gasped, and sniffed a tear or two away.

"What you've always wanted," he murmured. There were three buttons still fastened on the robe. He lost his patience with them. As he tugged, the remaining fasteners snapped off one at a time and went sailing across the room.

"Tell me to stop," he rasped. "It's your last chance."

"What I've always wanted?" Not a remonstrance, but a question asked in awe, as if a sudden need had come upon her and she could not understand what or why.

"What you've always wanted, woman." A tender smile crept across his craggy face, and then a look of surprise. "You never wear a bra?"

"I—never."

"Yes. I can see why," he murmured, his concentration now on the mounds of white flesh before him. A man would be a fool to ignore it all, he told himself.

He stood up and carried her to the couch across the room, and stretched her flat on her back.

"Charlie?"

"What, sweetheart?"

"I—you mean that?"

"Yes. We're going to get married, you and I. Want me to stop?"

"I don't know, do I?"

Charlie Mathers dropped to his knees in front of the couch. His eyes absorbed all the glorious womanhood of her, standing proud and firm. Gently he lowered his head, and allowed his tongue to possess one of those hard brown tips.

There's nothing new to all this, Rachel's analytical mind told her. I've seen movies of it being done, I've read books describing it. Nothing's new, but everything's new. The moment his mouth surrounded her nipple she had felt the involuntary contraction that brought her entire body into play. Nothing new? She drew a desperate breath, then locked one of her hands in his hair. Not for punishment, not for control, but rather to give herself something of him to hang on to while her world began to go around in circles.

Sweetheart? He called me sweetheart. Or is that just the normal line that a rampaging male uses to bring a woman to compliance? Probably that. Probably—but at that moment he surrendered his claim at her breast, and moved gently and slowly up her throat, across her chin, and up to her lips.

Leaving behind? A sort of regret that he had stopped. A coolness where his lips had been, as the air in the room absorbed the dampness he had left behind. A slight chill quickly replaced by his massaging hand as it climbed the mountain.

moment, then moving down and down as if he meant
jump into the canyon between her legs.

Rachel summoned all her strength and forced herself
ore frigidly into an unmovable statue—for about thirty
conds. His fingers moved again, over the cliff, into the
nyon. She had never dreamed such excitement could
ist. She had never known that that one little spot was
ere. He touched it gently, and Rachel Hammond
reamed in excitement, bounced in the bed and snatched
him as if she were trying to completely absorb him.
He moved then, nudging her legs apart and moving
between them. "Ready, Rachel!" She was shaking
th excitement, and he wanted to talk! I'll kill him, she
ld herself—just as soon as he's finished!

"I—I——" The words would not come. Perspiration
as pouring from her forehead.

"I understand," he said. Gently, still using one hand
tease her breasts, he settled his weight and entered
r. Rachel's world dissolved. Multicolored fireworks
re flashing around her head. Some fool was yelling,
Faster, faster!" That same fool reached madly for him,
ying to force him deeper when he was in his with-
awal cycle.

His huge hands slipped under her buttocks, synchro-
zing her movements with his. He pounded at her for
wild moment, and then took her with him up to the
max of the Little Death. After which he collapsed on
of her, panting, out of breath. As was she.

More than one minute passed, but Rachel was unable
measure time exactly. Her mind was still disconnected
the rest of her. He seemed to weigh a ton, but when
ied to move she clutched him tightly and murmured
ntic "No." More minutes. She could no longer feel

Lips. Gentle, caressing lips, touching once gently and
moving on, then coming back again to seal her entirely
within herself. Without thinking, she closed her eyes.
His tongue moved against her lips, nuzzling, seeking ad-
mission. Which she granted without protest. The lips
pressed more fully, the tongue sought—something. And
a violent ionic charge ran up and down her spine. She
wiggled closer, but by the time she found the better position his mouth had moved on. Back down to her breast,
a momentary halt, and then farther down into the soft
roundness where her waist constricted.

Somebody in the room moaned in excitement. Rachel
heard the sound, felt the excitement, and her whole body
quivered.

"Rachel? Shall I stop?"

She heard him as if from a distance, as if he were
standing by the top of an empty barrel, and she were
inside on the bottom. A hollow sound that reverberated
around the barrel and into both ears at the same time.
She was entirely confused.

"Rachel?"

"I—don't know," she gasped. And then, desperately,
"Don't stop!"

A hand and arm slipped under her at the knees;
another balanced her from behind her back. He lifted
her up as if she weighed nothing. Strange, she told herself
through the confusion. I feel like nothing. Is it possible
to float? Magic?

Somehow he opened the double doors of the living
room without shifting his hands. Somehow, although he
had never been there before, he found the turning and
opened her bedroom door. Somehow he stretched her
out gently on her bed and knelt beside her. Throughout

all of this Rachel Hammond had kept her eyes closed. Now she opened one eye.

His face was inches from hers, his eyes open and staring. There was an expression on his face that she had never seen before on any man. It was hard for her to study it with just one eye, but she dared not open the other, or surely the whole affair would disappear—fade away and disappear. So she searched his face carefully.

Desire? Yes, much of that. There was a darkening under his normal tan, and she could feel the heat arising even at this distance. Confidence? As if he knew he was doing what she wanted. As if he *knew* something that she did not know—as yet.

Love? She had never known love before, and could not judge.

And then he moved. Her robe slipped off her shoulders under his questing fingers. Her négligé followed. The room was cool. She shivered.

"I know, love."

His mouth again, at her breast, while one hand roamed up and down from neck to waist, searching for—all those little spots that caused her to quiver. Searching as if he were a hunter who knew where to go. And then, using his fingers like little soldier's legs, he marched one hand slowly down across her breast, into the deep declivity of her stomach, and then paused.

She was wearing a pair of very utilitarian white briefs. The Rachel Hammonds of this world paid no attention to things that others did not normally see. His fingers disappeared under the rim of those briefs. Rachel gasped and put her arms around him, trying to pull him closer.

His fingers stopped for a moment. Her briefs disappeared. He drew back. Disappointed, Rachel opened her eyes and wished for one wild moment that there might

be mirrors on the ceiling. Which was an imp[ossible] dream. But she could see herself, a pale white [figure] stretched out on top of the blue and white sprea[d that] covered the bed. Something moved in the corner [of her] eye. She turned to look. He was standing by the [bed,] completely nude himself.

Startled, Rachel turned away, and he laughe[d, a] humorous, teasing laugh. "Well, we can't all b[e as] beautiful as you." It was a lie, she told herself, beca[use] he's as beautiful as I am. Not the same, but beauti[ful.] She turned back, forcing herself to look.

He loomed over her while she searched him out. The[re] was a T-formation of light hair across his chest, left [to] right. From its midpoint another segment of ha[ir] marched down his flat stomach and into—oh, my, sh[e] told herself and shut her eyes. Oh, my!

Rachel stiffened from head to toes, her arms rigid [down] beside her, the fingers bent into fists, her nails bitin[g] into her palms. The bed under her swayed as he settle[d] beside her. She could feel the touch of him all along h[er] body. He's going to do it, she told herself fiercely. H[old] on tight. Maybe it won't hurt!

"Relax, woman." His head was at her ear. She u[nder]stood the words, but could not believe them. N[ever] in any of her research had she come across a[ny of] these exercises where one should "relax"!

"For God and England?" he murmured in[to her.] What in the world is he talking about? she ask[ed.] Get on with it. Why doesn't he get on with it?

But not in any manner that she might have [expected.] He chuckled again, lay down at full lengt[h by her,] and began to draw little circular diagrams [on her ex]posed body with his index finger. Gentl[y, over] hill and down dale—pausing at the top [of the]

the fullness of him inside her. Regret washed her mind clear. She opened her eyes and grinned at him.

"And is that," she asked coyly, "all there is to it?"

"Why, you little vixen," he said, laughing. He rolled off her, but not so far away as to be out of touch. "Yeah, that's all, lady. Thirsty?"

"As if I had been in the desert," she assured him. "You?"

"The same."

"There's a little refrigerator in the corner," she suggested. He rolled away from her, landing on hands and knees on the thick carpet. A moment later he was back with two iced glasses.

"What is it?"

"Bourbon and branch water," he said, laughing. "Well, I guess you don't have branch water in these parts. I salute you." He raised his glass. Rachel did the same. One sip to moisten her bone-dry lips, another to wet her throat, and then she held the glass up and played with the droplets that beaded its rim.

"It was—something different," she said with a sigh. "Has this been going on for very long?"

"Thousands of years," he returned as he finished off his drink and climbed back on the bed. "Thousands of years. God said 'increase and multiply.' So he made the sex game the most enjoyable item in all the world."

"But—so many people seem to have trouble with it."

"Yes. But not you and I, Rachel, thank the Lord. Yes, it's the only game that rich and poor alike can enjoy."

"Poor better than rich," she commented with a grin. "The poor people seem to do so much better at it than the rich."

"That's because they don't have as many hang-ups as
the rich," he said. "Now then, I've had a hard day, and
I could use a little nap. Drink up."

She did. He lay back in the bed and pulled her up
against him. And before she could think of the rest of
the stuff she wanted to talk about he was fast asleep.
She left him that way for about a half hour.

Is that all there is to it? she asked herself. Lord, that
was enough! She had never in all her life had such a
physical reaction as during that last climactic moment.
And there he lay, sprawled out on his back, making little
noises as he breathed in and out. Not a handsome face,
she reminded herself, but good enough to go the route.
A sturdy head, full of all kinds of thoughts, able to do
a million and one things that needed doing in this world.
A chest that moved up and down as he breathed—and
a scar just above his right nipple. Four inches or more
of scar. She caught her breath as she watched it. So recent
as to be still inflamed. Battle wounds?

You know so little about him, she told herself. So very
little. And you want to know so much. If my—she patted
her soft stomach and blushed—if my baby looks like his
father, wouldn't that be—nice?

He was stirring uneasily at the moment. She was
leaning over him, so close that one of her breasts was
rubbing across his midsection. Purely accidental, she told
herself as she straightened slightly. Is that how he's
turned on? Could he possibly do it again?

It didn't seem so. Could he do it again? Recklessly
she leaned over and extended a hand to just—touch,
that's all. Just touch.

His eyes popped open. "What the hell," he muttered
as he rolled over on top of her. Dismayed—and yet
pleased with herself—she discovered that he could.

*   *   *

"Now that's not the type of afternoon I had planned," he said, leaning back in one of the lounge chairs in the living room. "I hadn't expected to—have things explode in my face. Are you all right, Rachel?"

"All right? I couldn't be better. Well, that isn't exactly right. I can see I'd be better off if you had shaved this morning."

"My apologies. I usually get it done in the morning and, if I'm going out with a lady, again at night before we go. A hard business, being a man."

"Yes, I can see it must be." She giggled. "Very hard."

"Don't rub it in, woman. I've got more than one scratch on my back that I didn't put there. You were like a wildcat in that second session. Whatever happened to the sweet demure Hammond girl?"

"I wouldn't know," she told him. "I'm a little—sore—in one or two places. Somebody bit me—right on my—right there somewhere. But I'm glad we were able to do it. You really were the man I wanted." Her face turned brilliant red. I can't imagine doing—that—with Edward, she told herself. Or any other man I've ever met. Only with Charlie.

"And so that part of it is concluded," she said. There was just a little wistful touch in her voice.

"Concluded?"

"Well," she said, "once might be a miss, but twice is certainly going to achieve my goal, isn't it?"

"Oh, Lord, do you still have that on your mind?"

No, I hadn't, she told herself. From the moment he touched me, I haven't even thought about the consequences. But now that we are back to the rational, I can force myself to think. The baby is on the way, I've managed to get one project going down the road, so why shouldn't I boast about it?

"Is that really what you were thinking?" He had walked across the room and was standing directly in front of her, glaring down.

And now he's angry, she thought. I wonder why? We've both played our part, and the play is over, isn't it? Of course not, her conscience told her. Of course it's not over. He's a fine man, the kind of man my father would have just loved as his son.

As his son. The phrase stuck in her mind, wiping out every other thought. As his son. My father. My grandfather. In the end, Rachel Hammond, you have ended up by doing just what all those men wanted. Damn this male world!

"Yes," she said as she stood up gracefully. "I've got what I wanted." She patted her stomach to emphasize her mood. "Everything has turned out fine, and I enjoyed myself considerably in the doing. I do have to thank you for all that, Charlie."

"And now? Don't thank me so damn casually. We're going to get married, you and I, and between us raise this little fella the way he should be raised."

"Why, there isn't any 'you and I,'" she said recklessly. "I thought you understood that. I needed you desperately for the laying of the keel, but from now until the launching I can take care of things myself."

"You think so?" he asked harshly. "You think you've got everything sewn up, and now you can go off about your business?"

"Why, of course."

His face quivered, and then he smiled at her. Not a pleasant smile, but rather a cold thing, cold enough to freeze the Missouri River. "Don't be too sure about that," he said. "It's been known, lady, that it takes more than a couple of quickies before a woman becomes pregnant. You may find that nothing's working. Then where will you be?''

Oh, God, she thought, that couldn't be. We were a perfect match, he and I, and—no, the Lord wouldn't do a thing like that to me. He's just trying to frighten me. She plucked up her courage. There was no way in this world that she could do such a thing with anyone except Charlie, and he was getting up on his high horse!

"That's not possible," she told him, her eyes flashing the danger signal. "I'm sure it's not possible. I'm sure you've served your purpose."

"And we won't be needing each other any more?"

"And——" She didn't want to say it, but anger carried her forward. "And we won't be needing each other any more," she said. "Come by the office tomorrow, and I'll pay you off."

"The hell you say," he muttered. He took one step in her direction. She backed off. So did he. There was a perplexed expression on his rugged face. "Look at me, Hammond. You've only heard it a couple of times in passing, and I'll wager you don't remember. What's my full name?"

"Why—Charlie," she replied. And then puzzled through her mind, trying to remember the rest. Yes, he had said it one or two times out at the ranch, but now, for the life of her, she couldn't remember. "I—it just seems to have slipped my mind."

"Mathers," he told her. "Charlie Mathers. And there's no way you're going to avoid me or my name, love. You and I are going to be married. Sooner than later, because my grandfather isn't one to put up with that later business. Have you got that?"

"But——" He had used all the right words, Rachel told herself. No, I could possibly raise this child all by

myself, but—I don't want to! I want Charlie Mathers.
Day and night till death us do part. Even though he
means to be the boss? her conscience asked. Even if, she
thought. Even if.

He knew what she was thinking. Her flexible face had
raced through all the emotions of her internal argument.
"We're going to get married," he repeated.

Rachel found herself wrapped up in the middle of his
arms. "Yes," she murmured. The pressure of his arms
increased for a second, and then relaxed. His lips came
down on hers and sealed her to the bargain. For aeons
the wild, exhilarating kiss ran on, until finally he broke
it for lack of breath.

"There," he said, inhaling deeply. His arms opened
and Rachel, totally exhausted, dropped into the nearby
lounge chair.

"There indeed," she said. There hardly seemed to be
anything else to say. Married, she thought. Like thousands of other women throughout history. I never
thought it could happen to me. And happily ever after?

Charlie seemed to shrug all his muscles, and managed
to relax. Marriage, he thought. I've been avoiding it for
years, but now I've chased this woman until she caught
me. Who would have thought? In need of movement,
he walked over to the occasional table sitting by the
couch. A copy of the *National Gossiper* was lying there,
face down. The back page reminded him of what Frank
had said at the restaurant. He flipped the magazine over
so its cover could be seen. The story attracted him. He
picked up the publication and began to read.

"Lord," he muttered. "You people are giving this
poor soul a hard time. Embezzler, crook of the first
water. Who the devil is this man? Story on page four."
He flipped through the pages. "Ah, here we have it."

And a pause, while his anger built. "Dear God! Roger Borgen!"

He whirled around, folded the magazine neatly in quarters, and put it down carefully on the table. Rachel could see the rage rising in his eyes, the anger reflected in his carefully enunciated words.

"There's not a word of truth in this," he said harshly. "Don't you people ever check *anything* before you print it?"

Rachel looked up at him for a second, frozen in time. Then all her training took over, and it was Hammond who responded icily, "I haven't read this issue. But I'm sure that it's been investigated with our usual thoroughness. Who was the gentleman, did you say?"

"I'll say." His voice had dropped to a whisper. "The finest man I have ever known. Roger Borgen. You've just bet me a million dollars that there isn't a word of truth in this rag."

"I—Uncle Roger?" She drew herself up to her full height, her head spinning. "I don't remember making any such bets with you!"

Charlie looked down at his watch. His big hands were trembling. "By this time my lawyer will be down at the courthouse, filing a million-dollar suit against you and your paper. That's our bet, lady. I'm going to bust this filthy magazine of yours. When I get through with it, you'd better damn well pray I don't wreck your ranch as well."

"Others, better than you, have tried. None of them succeeded."

"Then listen carefully," he said. She shivered. His voice was deep, vibrant, threatening. "My name is Charlie Mathers. Charlie Mathers. And you're going to be seeing a lot of me, Hammond. You've stepped beyond

the bounds of decency this time. The reason why nobody
has ever beaten you before is because they didn't have
enough money and enough evidence. This time you've
bitten off more than you can chew. I've got the money,
and I'll get the evidence.'' He flipped the magazine over,
face down, and shoved it at her. And then he turned
and walked away, slamming doors as he went, leaving
her frozen, trembling.

Her mind whirled. He had come to ask her to marry
him, and he had left with a death wish in his mind. The
headline said,

Millionaire philanthropist might have been embezzler. Famous Libertyville tycoon being checked by
the Gossiper Spotlight Team. Details on page four.

The magazine slipped from her fingers and fell to the
floor.

''I suppose,'' she screamed in hysterical panic at the
door which had slammed behind him, ''this means the
wedding is off?''

''I was beginning to wonder what happened to you,''
Frank Losen said. He was sprawled out on Charlie's favorite couch, in the middle of Charlie's favorite
apartment. ''It's been a busy afternoon.''

''You can say that again,'' Charlie said as he closed
the door behind him. ''I'm exhausted.''

''Oh? How did you make out with Hammond? Did
you ask her?''

''Yeah.'' Charlie made for the bar and poured himself
a shot of rye. ''I asked her, and then I read that rotten
magazine cover!''

''And then?''

"Luckily there was a husky young man there I could use for practice. After I read that magazine I was almost sick to my stomach. I guess the wedding's off."

"You only guess?"

"Hey, you can't just turn off the tap," Charlie muttered as he refilled his glass. "Can you love a woman and hate her at the same time?"

"Damned if I know. Say, I managed to get a few things done," his lawyer told him. "First of all, the injunction was a cinch. The judge took one look at the headlines and signed the writ right away. We've locked up the garages, and all the trucks are under guard by my private agency."

"That's okay for next week," Charlie agreed. "But I want something—I want to smash that woman. Tomorrow."

"We might just do that, too." Frank Losen pulled up his briefcase and set it on the table. "I've managed to get a call out for a special meeting of the stockholders. For tomorrow, it's set. Over in the boardrooms at the pyramid."

"I don't quite—my mind's a little disturbed."

"It means that you can go into that meeting with enough proxies to toss her out on her ear, that's what it means."

"But hell, Frank. I can't run that magazine. If we throw her out the whole place will collapse."

"Maybe so, maybe not. There's Elmer Chatmas, you know. He's been in harness for so long I don't think he could ever quit. Elmer's a sensible man. He's been the power behind the throne for a long time. And I'm sure there must be one or two other people around who could help out?"

"I wouldn't know," Charlie said. "God, my head aches."

"Another afternoon at the bottle?"

"No, Lord, no. I wish it *was* that."

"I don't believe it. You, Charlie Mathers, *wishing* for a hangover?"

"There are some things, Frank, that you lawyers don't know. Shoeing a horse, for example, or——" He stopped at just the right moment. How would Frank ever understand the rest of the statement—*or loving a woman*?

"I suppose you're right," the lawyer said as he gathered up all his papers and stuffed them back into the briefcase. "I'll see you tomorrow, then. Ten o'clock?"

"Ten o'clock." Charlie walked him to the door and showed him out. And then he went over to the window and looked out over the city. "Libertyville, Kansas," he murmured. "Home of cows and printing presses and tornadoes and indomitable ladies." He shook his head dolefully. "And I don't know just which one of them makes for the biggest problem . . ."

Back to the cabinet, where he refreshed his rye and added an ice cube. Rachel Hammond! He settled back in his chair and considered. Out at the ranch she had been beginning to change. Oh, there had been times when she slipped back into her old form. But certainly there had been change. And now, to come back to the city and find her not only as bad as she had ever been, but even worse. If that were possible.

Tomorrow, he told himself, I'm going to rush into the meeting room and bring the whole house down around her head. And then? And then I'm going to go back to Texas and have a month of drink and destruction.

And then?

And then I'll scoot around and see if there's any country aching for a fight, looking for a competent fighter pilot! And with that he played chug-a-lug with his glass and threw the empty container at the artificial fireplace.

CHAPTER NINE

TOMORROW! Rachel Hammond eased back in her chair and sighed. Outside her office on top of the pyramid, a worker was cleaning the streets of the city, pounding water down on the mid-Kansas town as if there were to *be* no tomorrow. "So what are the possibilities?" She turned to look around the circle of her senior staff.

"Two different kinds of problem," Elmer said. "The injunction and the court suit are a problem, but not one that we haven't seen before. We go to court. We stall. We tell them that we have reason to believe—and all that junk. Then we offer to settle. In our next issue we publish a retraction—on the last page of the magazine, and in small print. If they persist we offer them money."

"And if they won't compromise, and they won't take the money?"

"That's what Zimmerman is for," Elmer said. "That's why we keep him on retainer. What say, lawyer?"

Alfred Zimmerman sat in the middle of the circle, a small, neat man, precise in all ways, wearing a pair of gold-rimmed spectacles. He cleared his throat, and tried not to look at Hammond. "I thought it was the policy," he said, "that all stories of probable risk would be reviewed by my staff? I didn't see this issue of the magazine until this morning at breakfast. I must say that you spoiled my meal."

"But it sold a lot of copies," Hammond said harshly. "Get on with it. What do we do next?"

"Well—as far as the injunction goes—we really need to find out who's behind all this. The court record indicates Frank Losen is suing, as trustee for the estate of Roger Borgen. Now, Mr. Losen is as shifty a lawyer as ever came out of Dodge City. But I can't believe that Frank is acting for the estate out of the goodness of his heart. I wish I knew who's backing him."

"And if we find that out?"

"Then we turn loose our team of investigative reporters and get a profile on this man. Who knows? *He* might be susceptible to all the foibles of mankind. A little adverse publicity might make him see reason."

"Dirty pool," Elmer chimed in. "That's what got us in this situation in the first place. More of it might croak us."

"But it's an angle, and we'll try it anyway," Rachel decided. "Next?"

"As for the other problem?" The lawyer set back in his chair and brushed his decidedly thin hair with one well-groomed hand. "We have a great deal more to fear from the meeting of the corporation than we do from the judicial system. Given the fact that everything possible is against us, I could still string out the court case for four or five years—maybe more. But the corporation?"

Rachel rubbed her forehead. It ached. All of her ached. But for good reason, she told herself. What a wonderful afternoon! Yes, Charlie left in anger, but I'm sure that once I get this problem with the magazine straightened out I can get Charlie back into focus. A great deal of man, Charlie. And I can't do without him!

Zimmerman was still droning on. Whatever he said went right past her ears and over her head, ignored. Charlie. She leaned back in her chair and closed her eyes.

Charlie on his gelding, riding through the prairie grass, a man in charge of a man's destiny. And if he could make the ranch pay she wouldn't need the *National Gossiper*—not for anything. She rubbed her hand over her forehead again. The ache persisted. But the conversation around her did not. Her eyes snapped open. They were all staring at her, waiting.

"Restate the problem," she ordered. Zimmerman shrugged his shoulders and fumbled back through the packet of papers he had before him. "Slim it down," she added. "I'm afraid that you've got into the habit of telling me more than I care to know."

Zimmerman was not the kind of man to blush. From an old German family, his folk had come to Kansas when it was still caught in the throes of the slave wars, the dark and bloody ground. But he *was* perturbed. He paused to clear his throat again.

"Simply stated, Hammond," he began, "you do not have absolute control of the stock in this corporation. Nobody has. When Roger Borgen died, he held some forty percent. You held some forty-two percent, and the rest—we just don't know where the rest of the stock is." Another stop to clear his throat. He reached into his waistcoat pocket and found a lozenge which he placed on his tongue.

"We have carefully avoided a corporate meeting for several years. In that way the legally elected board of directors could continue to function. Now, we are setting sail on a stormy sea——"

"Please, no rhetoric," Rachel said. "Can somebody find me an aspirin?"

A half-dozen hands moved to produce the pill. Rachel selected a couple and gulped them down.

"I don't know how you do that without water," Elmer commented.

"I don't know how you do that with alcohol," she said grimly. "Now, Mr. Zimmerman?"

"We could call a meeting," the lawyer said, just as grimly as she, "and find out that the holders of this missing stock could show up—and vote against us."

"Hmm." Hammond tapped her pencil on her desk top and suddenly noticed it was in disarray. It was something she hated. Desktops should be neat, tidy. And hers was not. She shut out the staff members and their comments and began to restore order to the scene in front of her. The staff grew quiet. They all knew what was going on. Even a paperclip out of order was usually the source of a maddening comment. But this time Hammond had nothing to say; she just sorted and shifted and pushed until things were as they should be. And only then did she turn back to her staff, most of whom were consulting their watches.

"So it's late," Rachel said. "And you're all tired— as I am. Well now." She ticked off the things to be done.

"You, Mr. Zimmerman, go back into court and see if you can get this temporary injunction lifted. Lie, cheat, steal—I don't care how you do it. I want the trucks to move tomorrow and the presses to roll." The lawyer nodded, replaced his papers in his briefcase, and started to get up.

"And you, Elmer. Take another press run of today's magazine, and move it to the rail head for shipment. I have the hunch that this thing will sell double our usual subscription list."

"No changes?" Elmer asked.

"Changes? Why changes?"

"I think," Elmer said, "we ought to add a little cover-box saying that people have got an injunction seeking to suppress this issue."

"Yeah," Hammond said, coming to life for the first time. "Freedom of speech. Freedom of the Press. Right on the first page. Fourteen point type. Go!"

They all moved to leave. A collective sigh could be heard from all around the room. The wall clock behind her struck eleven. "All but you, Harry."

The young man who was the magazine's auditor stopped and turned around with a question on his face. "Harry," she said softly, as the others hustled out, "I want you to spend the night or the week or the month, and get me a list of all those other stockholders. Name, address, telephone number. And call me the minute you know something, whether I'm at the office or at home. Don't fail me."

He smiled an acknowledgement and went rushing from the room. Hammond always rewarded those who did well for her. And who knew what sort of reward the Ice Lady might possibly distribute?

Rachel Hammond, who knew exactly what that grin intended, smiled herself and slumped back in her chair. Whatever the young man thought his reward might be, it wouldn't be what he hoped for. She leaned her head back in the big swivel chair and, not expecting to, she fell asleep.

It was a sleep filled with dreams. The same dream, actually, running through her mind as if it were a tape spliced in a circle for continuous running. In that dream she came up to the ranch house in her limousine, and climbed out, dressed in a pure white wedding gown. It was a full-figured gown, sweeping down from her hips to her feet in a wild explosion of silk and satin and orange

blossoms. She twirled a couple of times, but no dust
dared to rise. The bodice of the dress, reaching upward
from waist to choker collar, consisted of a single layer
of transparent silk. It came upward to her neck, where
a tiny rosebud was tucked into a frill of lace. Beneath
the skirt were two cotton petticoats that rustled whenever
she walked; above the skirt, under the bodice, there was
nothing but Rachel Hammond.

In her dream she walked toward the veranda; Charlie
came down the stairs, almost tripping over his spurs. He
was dressed in black dress pants, a handsome pair of
dark brown boots, and a big smile. Just the sight of him
excited her. Her breasts kept coming to attention,
pushing outward at the transparent silk. He reached out
his hands to her; she ran in his direction. Only when
they were but an inch or two away did his grin disappear. "Mathers," he said grimly, and then the rest of
him seemed to fade away, like the Cheshire cat of literary fame, but leaving behind that terribly grim face.
Until that too disappeared. A moment of blackout followed, and then the film began to run again.

Rachel awoke and screamed. The night cleaning lady
pushed in the door of her office and flipped on the light.
"You still here, Ms. Rachel? I thought everybody had
gone home long ago. Child, it's two o'clock in the
morning!"

"I—I must have been overtired," Rachel stammered.
"Everybody's gone? My chauffeur too?"

"Everybody gone, Ms. Rachel. I could get you a cab
real easy. There's a couple of them park right outside
the door most nights."

"I'd like that." Rachel stood and stretched. It was
true. Every bone in her body ached—especially her hip-

bones. He was a heavy man, she reminded herself, and giggled at the thought.

"You really must be tired," the cleaning woman said. "Here, let me help you to the door, and then I'll call downstairs to the night guard. He'll look after you—you need someone to, anyway."

Rachel readjusted her blouse and shook her skirt free. Wrinkles did not matter, not tonight. With her eyes only half open, she kept her right hand extended to the wall. The touch steered her—and reassured her. The little elevator waited for her. She climbed in and pushed the button. The car started, stopped, and started again, moving so slowly down the shaft that she almost fell asleep again. "I must get this thing fixed," she said, just as the lobby door opened.

"Does need some overhauling," the guard ventured. "I got one of those cabdrivers waiting for you, ma'am."

"Don't call me ma'am," she said, but gently. "Call me—Rachel. You're Foster, aren't you? What are you doing working the midnight shift? You've a wife and two children at home, I seem to remember."

"Three now," Foster said. "Night shift pays more money. Here you go. Slide into the cab and he'll take you straight home."

"I feel—as if I'd been on a wild drinking party," Hammond told the busy driver moments later. "But I haven't had a drop of alcohol. What do you suppose it is?"

"Release of tensions," the cab driver told her. "Happens all the time. I get all these big shots who come off the airplane filled with their fears and tensions, you know. And then, after the meeting's over and they're still employed, they just fall back in the seat of my cab. Some of them start singing."

"You wouldn't want me to sing," Rachel said. "Even the cows can't stand my singing. But Charlie, he sings like a bird. Well, at least the cows like him." A pause for reflection. "And I do too."

"And here's your hotel, ma'am. Not to worry about the fare. I run a tab for the *Gossiper* people. You sure work strange hours. And let me give *you* a tip. When you go in, they've a fine indoor swimming pool. Take a dip, then call—Charlie, was it?"

"Yes. Charlie."

"Call Charlie on the phone and tell him you love him!"

"What a good idea," she murmured as she wandered into the lobby and took the elevator up to the penthouse.

Waiting outside her hotel is the most stupid thought of the day, Charlie Mathers told himself. So you blew your top. What else did you expect of a wandering cowpoke? Yes, she was wrong. No, you were right, Charlie, boy. And look what being right gets you. She comes back to her hotel at two in the morning, looking as if she were three sheets to the wind, and you're parked over here for the past three hours, hoping you don't have to explain to the beat cop why you're there.

Why *are* you there? Here? Charlie shifted restlessly in the driver's seat of his Porsche. No matter where he searched, he couldn't find a cigarette. Not even an old butt stuffed in the back of the glove compartment. His nerves were aflame. And that's what you get when you give up smoking. Nothing seems to be coming out right with Rachel Hammond. A lovely woman. And instead of marrying her you give her a one-night stand. One-afternoon stand. Whatever.

Why didn't you say something like, "Rachel, I love you. Let's you and I get married"?

Why didn't you? Because she would probably have said no, and had you thrown out on your pretty little ear!

He stopped his fidgeting. A light had appeared in the window of the penthouse. He watched it, fascinated. At that distance he could see nothing more than the light. What could she be doing? What had taken her so long to get upstairs? Damn! He pounded with one fist on the steering wheel of the car.

"You waitin' for a street car?" A heavy voice at his ear, with a heavy Scandinavian accent.

"Oh, hello, Officer. I was just——"

"Talking to yourself," the burly policeman said. "I've been watching you on and off for almost twenty minutes."

Think fast, Charlie Mathers told himself. Think fast. "Well you see, Officer, it's this way. I'm a writer. Novels, you know. And I found myself stuck with one of the scenes in my manuscript, so I came out into the night air to talk my way through it——"

"And of course you've got a tape recorder to keep track of all that?"

As it happened, he did. His car had one of everything, as he pointed out to the cop. "And so you've solved your problem, and now you'll be on your way, right?"

"Well—I do have a couple more scenes to work out," Charlie said.

"But you'll do that at home, won't you? This is a restricted residential district, and we don't like strangers parked on the odd streets. Sir."

"I—yes. I was just going." He looked up to the lighted window one more time. The window had been half opened, and now there was a shadow, as if someone was standing just inside. Damn, he told himself as he started the engine. Like some puling schooboy. So I love the girl, no matter what the devil she does, I love her.

"I wouldn't wait too long," the officer reminded him.

"No. I won't." He shifted into gear and roared away from there like a dragon late for a fire storm. Behind him the policeman grinned as he tucked his complaint book back into his pocket.

Two blocks from where he started, Charlie Mathers finally came to and took his foot off the accelerator. Moving at something much closer to the speed limit, he found his way across town safely. Luckily.

His mind was not on driving. Not at all. His mind was on a beautiful, strong-willed woman, lying beside him on a wide bed, smiling at him. But he did get to the underground garage at his apartment house, and took the elevator up to the seventh floor. As he fumbled with his door keys, he could hear his telephone ring. Speed compounded the fumbling. When he finally got the door open he dashed across the living room to pick up the instrument—and heard only the dial tone. Whoever it was that was calling had given up the ship. And it *might* have been Rachel, he told himself disgustedly. Maybe she would call again?

He went back to close the outer door, then stripped, article by article, in the living room. But no amount of slow motion helped. The instrument remained silent. Maybe I should call her?

He looked at his thin gold wristwatch. Three in the morning? No time for calling now. It might be just the last straw if I got her out of bed at this hour. Drooping, dispiritedly, he administered a double Scotch and found his way to bed.

*   *   *

Well, why not? Rachel told herself as she strolled across the lobby of her hotel. Cabdrivers are all graduate psychologists, aren't they? The indoor pool was in a separate room just off the lobby. Lighted by small green bulbs along the waterline, it beckoned to her. She held a locker, with several swim suits. It took but a moment for her to change. The warning sign cautioned. There were no life guards on duty after eleven o'clock. But Hammond was a woman very sure of her skills, and willingly took risks. She walked up to the deep end and dived in.

Thirty minutes later, completely refreshed, ready for almost anything, she wrapped herself in a bath towel and rode the main elevator up to her own floor. Neither the night clerk or the elevator operator had a thing to say. Life was often like that when all around you knew the approximate size of your bank account.

She almost rang the doorbell, until she remembered that her maid would have long since fallen asleep. So instead she fished with wet hands through her capacious handbag and found her own key. Moments later, dripping on the carpet but not caring, she flicked on the lights and made herself a daiquiri.

The telephone set was positioned on an occasional table against the wall. She went over and opened one of the sliding windows and looked out over the city. Nothing was moving, except for the police car parked just at the edge of her view.

"What you ought to do, Hammond," she said conversationally, "is have a nice drink, and then call him up, and tell him how very sorry you are for making a world-class fool of yourself. Like the cabdriver said, he can't know you love him if you don't tell him, right?"

She sipped the sweet cocktail in her hand and shuddered. It was too sweet for the occasion. She pulled out the telephone directory. It took hardly a moment to reach the telephone exchange of his apartment building. She fumbled with words, making a dozen or more statements, any of which might do the trick. She could hear his phone being rung.

"Mr. Mathers doesn't answer," the operator told her.

"Ring him again," Rachel said, suddenly no longer relaxed. With the telephone in one hand and her drink in the other, she paced back and forth nervously.

"He still doesn't answer, ma'am."

"Please," she stammered. Suddenly this telephone call had become more important than anything else in all her life. "Please—one more time." She could hear the feedback of the ringing. On and on and on. A tear formed in one eye, and then another. "Oh, God, what have I done?" she muttered to herself as she hung up and went off to bed.

The minute her head hit the pillows she was asleep. An awkward, troubled sleep, with that same dream running through her mind, over and over and over.

Until her maid came in and woke her to the bright sunlight of her morning.

CHAPTER TEN

THE boardroom at the *Gossiper* building was ornate but small. The huge mahogany table seated only eight people. In the corner by the president's chair was a mahogany podium and lectern, complete with microphones. Frank Losen nudged his client. "Like the British Parliament," he whispered. "Fifty members and only eight seats. That tells you something."

"Oh? What?" Charlie Mathers settled into his seat and tried to get comfortable. In honor of the occasion he was wearing an off-white suit, complete with a white shirt and a string tie. His lawyer, perhaps showing more knowledge, came in a pair of jeans and an open-necked shirt. The meeting had been called for eleven o'clock. They had arrived at ten-forty-five, and no one else was in the room.

"That shows you that Hammond-Borgen are not encouraging a large number of stockholders to have their say."

"I wish they'd turn their air conditioners down," Charlie mumbled. "I didn't get a lot of sleep last night. I could catch up on some here if it wasn't so darn cold."

"I hear that Hammond likes it that way." The lawyer opened his stuffed briefcase and handed Charlie a set of forms. "Your voting certificates," he said. "I get to vote your uncle Roger's stock, since the will has not yet been probated. You get to vote this proxy for your grandfather's shares in the blind trust. Altogether, we're sitting on a majority. You can vote Hammond out in one ballot.''

"Yeah," Charlie said as he hunkered down in his chair. What was that you told yourself yesterday? Voting Hammond out is the same as breaking her willpower. If I do, she'll collapse. And probably hate me for the rest of her life! How's about *that* for a cheery little vote?

Just to change the subject he asked, "How did things go in court today?"

"Not bad, not good," Frank said. "The judge refused to dissolve the injunction, but he also refused to make it permanent. And then he asked for supporting documents. You wouldn't believe the number of papers the corporation filed. It would seem that our sole interest in this suit is to stifle the free Press. That's a classy counteraction. They submitted so much material that it took the entire session just to identify the papers.''

"That sounds like a big-time job," Charlie retorted. "Can they get away with it?"

"It's all a ploy," Frank told him. "On our way out of the court their lawyer cornered me. He wanted to remind me how long such a suit could last. Then he said, 'I suppose I could talk Hammond into a settlement.' And he walked out."

"Settlement?"

"No, huh?"

"I—really don't know, Frank. I'm not much for these things. I need to be outdoors in the fresh air. And damned if I don't think I'd get along better with cows than with people. Hey, here they come."

Here they came indeed. A phalanx of people, all armed with briefcases and papers, marching in smartly to what were designated seats and standing areas, and clustering there. Including the two right behind Charlie, who gave him a dirty look, as if he had stolen their seats. He chuckled to himself, shrugged, and sat up taller than before. "Pull in your gut, Frank," he whispered. "We're on parade."

"Not me," Frank said as he slumped just a little further down in his chair. "I left the army twenty years ago. You don't put me back in harness by a little sideshow."

An elderly man near the head of the table was obviously counting heads. "That's Elmer Chatmas, the editor," Frank whispered. The counter seemed to be satisfied. He turned and nodded to a hulking man standing in the far front of the room. "And that's one of her guard dogs," Charlie whispered back.

The bulky young man opened the door. "No clash of cymbals," Frank whispered mockingly. Rachel Hammond was standing at the door. "For effect," Frank added.

"Oh, shut up," his client told him in an undertone.

He didn't want conversation. He just wanted to look. Or perhaps get up and run across the room and sweep her up and——

And at that moment Hammond came into the room. There was a hushed murmur of approval. Rachel Hammond had put off her business uniform. No navy blue skirt, no frilled blouse, no suit coat. Instead she was dressed in as simple a dress as woman could find. An A-line, lily white, with insets of bunches of little gold flowers embroidered around the hem. Charlie took a hissing deep breath. His companion, smiling, turned to stare at him.

She looks sweet enough to eat, Charlie thought. Magnificent. Beautiful. Thirty? Not possible. Twenty-one at the most. Simple, innocent. None of her tortured soul showed through the smile she flashed at him. There was some sort of message in that smile, only Charlie Mathers was in head over heels, and the message escaped him.

Rachel Hammond was smiling, indeed. But it was a smile she had to hold on her face with all her might, for fear that it would slip away and be carried down in a flood of tears. He looked so grand. Neat enough to grace any boardroom—or bedroom, she told herself. Isn't it strange? There isn't another person in the room. Not anyone. How easy to fall in love; how hard to do anything about it!

She walked over to the head chair in her usual graceful movement, swaying slightly, sending her skirt into a gentle arc. His eyes followed her every step. Her eyes were glued to his. If only he would smile.

And when he did her own smile became broader and more natural. She beamed at him, almost ignoring Elmer, who was holding her chair. The editor cleared his throat, bringing her back to reality. She offered him a smile as well, and slipped into her chair.

A throne, actually. Her father had had it specially built for her, with some four inches of extra height so she could look down at most other people at the table. Most people. Not him. His crinkly little smile indicated that he spotted the deception and acknowledged it. Rachel blushed and lowered her long eyelashes.

The chairwoman's gavel lay just within the perimeter of her sight. Nudged by Elmer, she picked it up and whacked it resoundingly on the block. It made an echo run through the room. There had been little sound before; now there was absolute silence.

"The secretary will read the purpose of this call for a special meeting of the board," Rachel said.

Halfway down the table a young lady, not more than twenty herself, managed to stand up nervously. "Madame Chairwoman, the board is in receipt of a letter from Mr. Frank Losen, holder of record of forty percent of the voting stock of the Hammond-Borgen Corporation, acting as executor of the estate of Mr. Roger Borgen. The calling makes reference to the issue of the *National Gossiper* of Monday last, and asks that a vote of no confidence in the present administration be taken."

"And that's all?" Rachel managed to keep her voice as cool and composed as usual. Somewhere in this room disaster lurked, and she had a good idea in which corner it was to be found.

"Yes, ma'am." Rachel motioned for her to be seated. The girl dropped in her chair as if a huge weight had been taken off her shoulders.

"Discussion?"

Elmer Chatmas got up and was recognized. "In every magazine there are some bobbles and breakdowns," he said. "Yet you will notice that over the past three years, while Hammond has been at the controls, the net profits of this corporation have increased more than fourteen percent. And that in a falling market. I can't believe that the needs of the organization can be best served by replacing Ms. Rachel." He sat down in a spurt of polite applause.

Frank Losen looked over at Charlie; he nodded negatively. Frank got up and was recognized. "Madame Chairwoman," he said, "we have not come here to measure how many dollars and cents this administration has made. We are here to defend a reputation. Most of you knew Roger Borgen well. He was a good, sincere man. In the last issue of our magazine we turned on him like a pack of wolves, cutting him up into little pieces. Uncle Roger—most of you called him that—was not an embezzler. He was not a crook. Instead he was a man of great and good proportion, a churchman of good repute, and a wise adviser. The only derogatory thing I ever heard said about Roger is that he was a lousy golfer. Acting for the estate of Roger Borgen, I demand a vote of no confidence in the existing board." He sat down. Only one pair of hands applauded. Charlie Mathers. And then silence.

Rachel stood up. "I know it's not proper for the chairwoman to enter the argument," she said softly. All in the room leaned forward to catch her words. "Mr. Borgen—you were right, Mr. Losen. Uncle Roger— Uncle Roger was the sweetest and kindest man I ever knew. Only, my father hated sweetness and kindness. And he taught me the same. The issue of which you speak was ordered by me. I ordered it, and then failed to check it. It said exactly what I wanted to have said. In every little detail."

There was a brief pause as she looked around the room.

She stabbed at her leaky eyes. "I am my father's daughter," she continued. "And I have never been more ashamed of myself than I am today."

A rustling of papers indicated the surprise of all the participants. Rachel seized the beveled edge of the table to steady herself. "You have seen the last issue of the *National Gossiper* in its present form. It is the determination of the present executive body to convert our magazine to a more gentle form. A magazine for women, without all the vitriol."

She stopped for a moment to wipe a tear which had escaped. "We will undoubtedly never again make the profits we have in the past. But profits are not everything." Another tear missed her handkerchief.

She slammed the gavel down. "Vote," she demanded. There was a croak in her throat as she wiped the tears and fell into her seat.

Elmer Chatmas stood up again. The dumpy old man looked confused, but he went about his work with a flat voice and a neutral face. "The administration votes forty-two percent of the outstanding stock of this corporation. Our vote is 'No.'"

Frank Losen sprang to his feet. In comparison to Elmer, the lawyer looked fit to fight. And he said so. "I vote the forty percent stock of the estate of Roger Borgen. I vote 'Yes.'"

The people at the table looked at each other uneasily. Rachel bowed her head and let her hair fall over her eyes. An occasional sob still broke through. It was the only sound in the entire room.

I know he has the rest of the stock, Rachel thought as she scanned Charlie's rugged face. I know he has it, and I know he'll vote against me. And then what will I do? All of my life, all of my being are tied up in this corporation—and I have used that power vindictively. I deserve to be fired, she told herself angrily—only—what shall I do afterward? Return to the ranch which I've already proved I don't know how to run? Abandon Kansas and go east? There might be something I can do—but I don't know what it is! Unconsciously, her hand dropped to her stomach and gently caressed the "perhaps" in her life. And that was the moment that Charlie Mathers stood up.

Every head in the room turned in his direction. He looked at them all slowly, one at a time. "A great wrong has been done, and it must be righted," he said. Faces fell in all directions. Only Frank Losen was smiling. Grinning, actually.

"But," Charlie said in his deep voice, "this is not the way to make things right. Eighty-two percent of the stock has been voted. I hold the proxy for fourteen per cent of the remaining stock, owned by my grandfather, Brigadier General Frank Hammond, and made a part of his blind trust." Another pause while he looked down at the papers in front of him.

"Madame Chairwoman," he said, "I abstain."

There was a scream of noise. Everyone in the room had something to say—to their neighbors, to their opposites, to themselves. But when Charlie Mathers dropped back into his chair, Frank Losen studied his face. "So that's the way the cookie crumbles?"

"That's the way, Frank."

"It's your cookie. I've got another court appearance this afternoon. See you around, shall I?"

"Sooner or later. Thanks, old buddy—for everything."

Frank Losen got to his feet, stuffing his briefcase with unused papers. "No thanks necessary," he said, chuckling. "Wait until you see my bill!"

Losen was the last to go. Except for Rachel, who was still huddled in her chair, and Charlie, who was just getting up to walk to the other end of the table. He disturbed the symmetry of things by pulling Elmer's chair over beside the huddled woman.

She looked up when he took her hand and began to caress it. "Why, Charlie?"

"Because that's the way I think things ought to be," he murmured. "Because there is no one in this state who could run the corporation better. Because you have finally come out from behind your Dr. Jekyll disguise, and into the real world."

"Not without help," Rachel said. "Not without help. Only now I feel as if there's nothing more for me to do. I don't really want to run the magazine any more, Charlie." She looked up at him. Tears had ruined her mascara, and she didn't care. He whipped a massive handkerchief out of his inside coat pocket and offered it to her.

"There's no real need for you to run this darn thing," he said finally. "I'm sure we could find someone else we could hire to keep it going. But not until we get an apology out for Uncle Roger."

"The apology is easy," she said, working up a little smile. "But what is all this 'we' business?"

"Not the royal we," he said. "The partnership we. You and I, Rachel. We are going to get married, and then we are going to—raise a few more members for our partnership. You don't mind?"

"Get married? I hadn't ever thought about that lately," she said. Only all of last night, and the night before, and perhaps a week or more out at the ranch. "But the more I think of it the better it sounds. We? The two of us? You don't plan to dictate to me the way my father did to my mother?"

"Not a chance." He leaned over and, almost as if it were simple, picked her up and settled her in his lap. "Not a chance." She shifted around until she was comfortable, and then turned her face up to him. He needed no further invitation. The door opened about halfway through the kiss.

"Oh. Excuse me." Rachel sat up, embarrassed. It was the same cleaning woman who had interrupted her the evening before. "There," said the beaming old lady, "I told you so, didn't I?"

"You surely did," Rachel said, smiling.

"Told you what?" Charlie asked.

"None of your business," they told him simultaneously.

CHAPTER ELEVEN

WHEN they came back from their ride Rachel was red-faced from the wind, and happy. They stabled both horses, wiped them down, and gave each of them a pail of oats. "You know," she said as they worked together, "you never did tell me what happened to Mr. Hendrix."

"Your old foreman? He comes up for trial on the first of September, charged with rustling and embezzling. The other pair of riders that worked for him, the judge gave each a suspended sentence and told them to get out of Kansas. Satisfactory?"

"I don't know," she said, sighing. "Mr. Hendrix worked for our family for so many years."

"So when the trial comes up you can be his character witness."

"You're teasing me!"

"Not a bit. A good word from a good woman could work a lot of good for him when he's being sentenced."

She thought for a moment, nibbling on her lip. "Then I will," she said, and took his arm for the walk back to the house.

But there was more to worry her and, being by nature a worrier, she picked at him. "You're sure that the Reverend will be here on time?"

"That makes six times you've asked," he said. "The answer is still 'yes.' He's bound to be!"

"But it's a long way from Texas, love."

"Not to my grandfather. Juarez Joe is flying him in. Or didn't you notice that we've cleared an airstrip in back of the house?"

"Oh, I noticed, but—it's a very important day, Charlie."

"I know, I know. And you were the woman who didn't want to get married."

"That was before I found out how much fun it would be. You *have* enjoyed it, haven't you?"

"Very much so."

Mrs. Colchester, who had begged to be returned to work, came into the room carrying a little white plastic container.

"Keep it at room temperature for thirty minutes," the cook said.

"Good." Rachel moved over to the table where the light was the strongest, and set up a little chemical laboratory of her own.

"And may I ask?"

"None of your business—yet," she told him. "Move out of the light, please. And be careful of that container! Good Lord, you gave me the darnedest scare. Spill that and I'd have to get a new kit and try it again tomorrow."

"Oh?" He picked up the little container and sniffed at it.

"Don't do that," she snapped at him. "Put it down. You can't imagine how much trouble it was getting that into the cup."

"Well, I can see it would be hard," he sympathized. She gave him another sharp look.

"You know what that is?"

"Yes, I know what that is. No, I don't know what you're up to with it. But go ahead anyway."

"Charlie!"

"What have I done wrong?"

"You just don't say that kind of thing. It isn't—isn't done."

"In the air force it's done all the time," he told her, and grinned as he did. "Don't be so sensitive, love. People have bodily functions, and those functions have names. Blame the problem on Queen Victoria. She's the one who cut all those useful names out of the language. After we get three or four kids around the house, you'll find that you need some short little word to use. Have you ever tried to teach a two-year-old kid to say 'Urinate'? Nonsense. So what are you going to do next?"

"Men," she muttered. "I don't know how I'm going to get along with you. Now if you'll stop bothering me, I have to follow the directions carefully. Let me see, now. First I take the test tube with the white powder in it, and I use this dropper to soak up some—fluid. And then I squeeze the fluid in with the powder."

"No trouble there," Charlie said. "Even I could do it."

"They have them in the high schools now," Mrs. Colchester contributed. "Kansas is a very advanced place."

"Well, then, Doctor?"

"Then I take this little plastic gadget with the two little bulbs in it, and put that in the mixture, and use it to stir things around until the powder all dissolves. After which I leave the bulbs in the liquid for fifteen minutes."

"All very educational," he said. "Just what are we supposed to learn from all this?"

"Why don't you read your paper?" Mrs. Colchester suggested. She brought it to him, gave him a little push, and settled him into the overstuffed chair.

"Well, thank you," he said, as he reached for the sports page.

"You're really not interested?" Rachel asked.

"Of course I am," he said sarcastically. "And I know you'll tell me all I need to know when you get finished there."

"You know, you're a pretty obnoxious man." Rachel checked her watch and went back to her little laboratory. Mrs. Colchester picked up the directions and read them to her.

"First, to wash off the bulbs in cold tap water. Do not touch the beads with the fingers."

"Okay. Next?"

"Next you take the cover off the tube with the colorless liquid, then you put the beads in that tube—and leave them there for fifteen minutes."

"I wish I'd had dinner," Charlie grumbled.

"Keep talking and you'll get nothing but bread and water," Rachel told him. "Look, Mrs. Colchester, only five minutes and already there's——"

"Fifteen minutes," the cook insisted. "We can't do this by guesswork. It works like a recipe. I tell you what. I sing you a little Indian song, huh?"

"So why not?" Charlie commented. "She sings better than either of us." He slapped the paper down on the table. "Would you believe it, the Royals baseball team lost another game. That means six losses and one win in the past two weeks. What they need is some young blood."

"You said it," Rachel yelled, holding up the tube with the two little bulbs within. "You said it! We did it!" Both women shouted their glee and danced each other around the table.

"Would you mind telling me what this is all about?" Charlie asked. "I'm really getting hungry."

"Settle back," Rachel told him. "Get a good grip on yourself. Ready?"

"Of course I'm ready," he grumbled. "I'm a former fighter pilot. Nothing really surprises me."

"Thank God for that," Rachel told him solemnly. "Charlie Mathers, you are about to become a father!"

"What?" Charlie Mathers, experience and all, stumbled to his feet, swayed slightly, and reached out to lean on his wife-to-be. "What?"

"Coward," she told him, and then squeezed him gently. "This is one of those early pregancy tests. See, the lower bulb has turned green."

"And so has Mr. Charlie." Mrs. Colchester giggled.

"And don't for heaven's sake tell my grandfather about the baby," he told her as they watched the two-engine Caravan circle the landing strip. Rachel was already in her wedding gown, a dainty white lace and silk concoction that fell barely to her heels. It hugged her from neck to waist, and then swept out in a voluminous skirt, fleshed out by a pair of starched cotton petticoats that provided the necessary rustle as she moved. The collar was high, Edwardian, with her hair carefully put up to match, and held up by a crown of orange blossoms. On her bosom she wore his wedding gift, a sparkling star sapphire, and on her right wrist was a bracelet of flowers. All in all, Rachel told herself, I feel very—bridish?

"That makes four times you've told me," she said mischievously. "And don't you tell him that you and I have been living out here for the past two weeks, either. I think that might be too much for an elderly Methodist minister."

The welcome was effusive. All of them walked back up to the house, where the old man allowed that he would love a cup of coffee, and then he sat down in the most commanding chair in the kitchen. "Now," he said, "you're a cute little thing, Rachel Hammond. So when is the baby due?"

Behind his grandfather's back, Charlie Mathers choked on his own coffee, and spilt a copious amount of the hot liquid over his hand. "Oh, I don't exactly know," Rachel said nonchalantly. "Perhaps in seven months. Something like that."

"If it's a girl," the old man said, "I hope it turns out to be as pretty as its mother."

"And if it's a boy?" she asked.

"Then," he said, "you'll have to try again."

Rachel managed a nervous smile. This tall old man, inches taller than his grandson, and only slightly bent with age, was a force she dared not trifle with. And yet there was something he had to know. "About the magazine," she offered.

He shifted his weight in his chair and half turned in her direction. "Yes," he said. "What about the magazine?"

"Well," she stammered. "I've—given it up."

"There's one good step."

"And Elmer Chatmas will run it."

"And that's another good step."

"And we thought—well, we won't take out the man from Mars thing, or the UFOs. But we thought we'd turn it around towards humor—and modern women. Kansas has a thousand writers with a good sense of humor. We're going to hire some of them, and let them go whichever way they want."

"And that," the old man said, "is another good step." There was a bustle in the living room as the rest of the guests arrived. Grandfather Mathers stood up, tall and sturdy in his eighty-seventh year. "Come on," he commanded, "let's get this show on the road."

The living room had been decorated—swamped, the word should have been—with all the flowers the Kansas summer could provide. A good half-dozen women from the magazine had undertaken the decorations. Mrs. Colchester had drafted help from the Potowotami Indian nation, who arrived *en masse* with piles of food.

"I hope I do this right," Mrs. Colchester murmured. "I never been a bridesmaid before. What do you think about that?"

"Don't ask me," Rachel said soberly. "I've never been a bride before."

"Nervous?" Frank Losen was the best man. They were standing together in a little group at the entrance to the living room.

"Scared to death," Rachel said, and bit her lower lip to hold on to her courage.

"About what?"

"That's the problem. I don't know what I'm scared about." I need something, she told herself desperately. I need some word, some phrase, some idea that ties us all, Charlie and I and all the others, into a viable, loving whole. What can I say?

Grandfather Mathers came into the room at that moment. No longer the big, casual man, but clothed now in his robes, his face calm and solemn. "So that," the good Reverend said, "leaves all the rest of it to us." He managed to drive the four of them into a group at the improvised altar. Almost it seemed as if he was herding them, as if they were a quartet of heifers. Then

he stepped around in front of them, inspecting everything with an eagle eye. He shrugged his shoulders and
managed to stand an inch or two taller, fingering the
bible he had used for seventy years.

"Dearly beloved," he said.

Yes, that's it, Rachel Hammond told herself excitedly. Dearly beloved! She looked up at the man who
stood beside her, and he returned the look. His lips
moved without speaking. "Dearly beloved," he
mouthed. Rachel Hammond, all her doubts resolved,
squeezed her man's arm and turned back toward the
preacher.

Those opening words floated out over the crowd,
leaked through the windows, and blessed the house and
all who would be its inhabitants. Rachel Hammond
missed all of the words that followed. There seemed to
be a protective blessing over the house and all the hearts
that would live in it. A blessing which released all her
real and fancied tensions, which erased all the memories
her father had pounded into her, so she could even think
of that man with equanimity.

"And I now pronounce you man and wife." The final
curtain. Rachel Mathers turned to look up at the huge
man standing beside her, drawing her to him with the
strength of his eyes alone. Promising the world and all
its appurtenances. The flower that was her heart opened
and burst into blossom. That's it, she told herself excitedly. My dearly beloved.

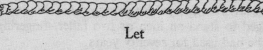

Take 4 bestselling love stories FREE

Plus get a FREE surprise gift!

Special Limited-time Offer

Mail to Harlequin Reader Service®

> 3010 Walden Avenue
> P.O. Box 1867
> Buffalo, N.Y. 14269-1867

YES! Please send me 4 free Harlequin Romance® novels and my free surprise gift. Then send me 6 brand-new novels every month, which I will receive months before they appear in bookstores. Bill me at the low price of $2.44 each plus 25¢ delivery and applicable sales tax if any*. That's the complete price and—compared to the cover prices of $2.99 each—quite a bargain! I understand that accepting the books and gift places me under no obligation ever to buy any books. I can always return a shipment and cancel at any time. Even if I never buy another book from Harlequin, the 4 free books and the surprise gift are mine to keep forever.

116 BPA ANRG

Name	(PLEASE PRINT)	
Address	Apt. No.	
City	State	Zip

This offer is limited to one order per household and not valid to present Harlequin Romance® subscribers. *Terms and prices are subject to change without notice. Sales tax applicable in N.Y.

UROM-94R   ©1990 Harlequin Enterprises Limited

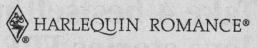

HARLEQUIN ROMANCE®

Question: What will excite & delight Debbie Macomber's fans?
Answer: A sequel to her popular 1993 novel,
READY FOR ROMANCE!

Last year you met the two Dryden brothers, Damian and Evan, in
Debbie Macomber's READY FOR ROMANCE. You saw Damian fall in
love with Jessica Kellerman....

Next month watch what happens when Evan discovers that
Mary Jo Summerhill —the love of his life, the woman who'd
rejected him three years before—isn't married, after all!

Watch for READY FOR MARRIAGE: Harlequin Romance #3307
available in April wherever Harlequin books are sold

If you missed READY FOR ROMANCE, here's your chance to order:

#03288   READY FOR ROMANCE   Debbie Macomber $2.99 ☐

(limited quantities available)

TOTAL AMOUNT	$
POSTAGE & HANDLING	$
($1.00 for one book, 50¢ for each additional)	
APPLICABLE TAXES*	$ _____
TOTAL PAYABLE	$ _____
(Send check or money order—please do not send cash)	

To order, complete this form and send it, along with a check or money order for the
total above, payable to Harlequin Books, to: **In the U.S.:** 3010 Walden Avenue,
P.O. Box 9047, Buffalo, NY 14269-9047; **In Canada:** P.O. Box 613, Fort Erie, Ontario,
L2A 5X3.

Name: _____
Address: _____ City: _____
State/Prov.: _____ Zip/Postal Code: _____

*New York residents remit applicable sales taxes.
  Canadian residents remit applicable GST and provincial taxes.

HRRFM

When the only time you
have for yourself is...

Spring into spring—by giving yourself a March
Break! Take a few *stolen moments* and treat yourself to a Great Escape. Relax with one of our brand-
new stories (or with all six!).

Each STOLEN MOMENTS title in our
Great Escapes collection is a complete and never-
before-published *short* novel. These contemporary
romances are 96 pages long—the perfect length
for the busy woman of the nineties!

Look for Great Escapes in our
Stolen Moments display this March!

SIZZLE by Jennifer Crusie
ANNIVERSARY WALTZ
by Anne Marie Duquette
MAGGIE AND HER COLONEL
by Merline Lovelace
PRAIRIE SUMMER by Alina Roberts
THE SUGAR CUP by Annie Sims
LOVE ME NOT by Barbara Stewart

Wherever Harlequin and
Silhouette books are sold.

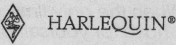 **HARLEQUIN®**

Don't miss these Harlequin favorites by some of our most distinguished authors!
And now, you can receive a discount by ordering two or more titles!

HT#25409	THE NIGHT IN SHINING ARMOR by JoAnn Ross	$2.99	☐
HT#25471	LOVESTORM by JoAnn Ross	$2.99	☐
HP#11463	THE WEDDING by Emma Darcy	$2.89	☐
HP#11592	THE LAST GRAND PASSION by Emma Darcy	$2.99	☐
HR#03188	DOUBLY DELICIOUS by Emma Goldrick	$2.89	☐
HR#03248	SAFE IN MY HEART by Leigh Michaels	$2.89	☐
HS#70464	CHILDREN OF THE HEART by Sally Garrett	$3.25	☐
HS#70524	STRING OF MIRACLES by Sally Garrett	$3.39	☐
HS#70500	THE SILENCE OF MIDNIGHT by Karen Young	$3.39	☐
HI#22178	SCHOOL FOR SPIES by Vickie York	$2.79	☐
HI#22212	DANGEROUS VINTAGE by Laura Pender	$2.89	☐
HI#22219	TORCH JOB by Patricia Rosemoor	$2.89	☐
HAR#16459	MACKENZIE'S BABY by Anne McAllister	$3.39	☐
HAR#16466	A COWBOY FOR CHRISTMAS by Anne McAllister	$3.39	☐
HAR#16462	THE PIRATE AND HIS LADY by Margaret St. George	$3.39	☐
HAR#16477	THE LAST REAL MAN by Rebecca Flanders	$3.39	☐
HH#28704	A CORNER OF HEAVEN by Theresa Michaels	$3.99	☐
HH#28707	LIGHT ON THE MOUNTAIN by Maura Seger	$3.99	☐

Harlequin Promotional Titles

#83247	YESTERDAY COMES TOMORROW by Rebecca Flanders	$4.99	☐
#83257	MY VALENTINE 1993	$4.99	☐
	(short-story collection featuring Anne Stuart, Judith Arnold, Anne McAllister, Linda Randall Wisdom)		

(limited quantities available on certain titles)

	AMOUNT	$
DEDUCT:	**10% DISCOUNT FOR 2+ BOOKS**	$
ADD:	**POSTAGE & HANDLING**	$
	($1.00 for one book, 50¢ for each additional)	
	APPLICABLE TAXES*	$ _____
	TOTAL PAYABLE	$ _____
	(check or money order—please do not send cash)	

To order, complete this form and send it, along with a check or money order for the total above, payable to Harlequin Books, to: **In the U.S.:** 3010 Walden Avenue, P.O. Box 9047, Buffalo, NY 14269-9047; **In Canada:** P.O. Box 613, Fort Erie, Ontario, L2A 5X3.

Name: _____

Address: _____ City: _____

State/Prov.: _____ Zip/Postal Code: _____

*New York residents remit applicable sales taxes.
 Canadian residents remit applicable GST and provincial taxes.

HBACK-JM